ALL WE LEFT BEHIND

Virginia Reed and the Donner Party

NANCY HERMAN

ISBN-13: 9781490317793
ISBN-10: 1490317791

Library of Congress Control Number: 2013915200
CreateSpace Independent Publishing Platform
North Charleston, South Carolina

Distributed in the USA

Cover Art by Victoria Faye Alday

To Tom, who kept listening.

ACKNOWLEDGMENTS

Writing may be a lonely endeavor, but the luckiest of us have supporters cheering us on from the sidelines.

All We Left Behind: Virginia Reed and the Donner Party would not have been completed without the unflagging enthusiasm of my family: Tom Herman, Eric and Jennifer Crippen, Emily Shotwell, and Brant Boivin. Thank you all for your love and support.

My talented writing friends offered comments and encouragement along the way. Many thanks to first readers Jeanne Ashcraft, Susan Britton, Randall Buechner, William Mueller, Elizabeth Varadan, and Naomi Williams. Additional thanks to later readers Rachel Dillon, Angelica Jackson, Christina Mercer, and Joe Vollmer.

I am especially grateful for the valuable editorial advice I received from Ellen Dreyer, Sands Hall, Mandy Hubbard, and Liza Ketchum.

A special thank you goes to Donner Party historian Kristin Johnson for her invaluable feedback, and to all the research librarians, museum curators, and national park and visitor center employees along the Donner Party route who aided me in my research.

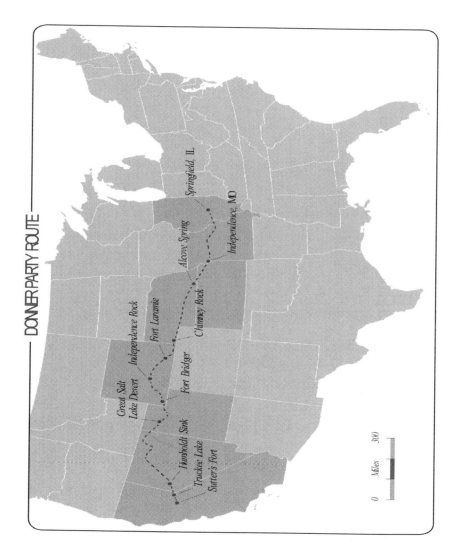

DONNER PARTY ROUTE

Springfield, IL

Alcove Spring

Independence, MO

Independence Rock

Fort Laramie

Chimney Rock

Great Salt
Lake Desert

Fort Bridger

Humboldt Sink

Truckee Lake

Sutter's Fort

0   Miles   300

"O Mary I have not wrote you half of the truble we have had but I hav Wrote you anuf to let you know that you dont know whattruble is.... "

—*Virginia Reed, in a May 1847 letter to her cousin Mary Keyes, after reaching California.*

PROLOGUE

*I*n my dream I was still cold, even though it was summer and I was back on the plains. Billy was there, sleek and spirited, galloping through the tall grasses. The Sioux boy was astride him, bareback, his hands wound deep into Billy's mane.

"You found my pony," I cried out.

The boy reined Billy in and lifted his head. His eyes searched the horizon.

"Puss. Wake up." Charlie's voice.

The Sioux boy caught my eye and waved. Then he and Billy began to fade away.

"Don't go," I called.

Someone was shaking me. "I can't wake her." Mama's voice rose. "I can't wake her, Charlie!"

"Please don't go," I whispered.

Billy and the Sioux boy vanished.

The daylight hurt my eyes. Mama and Charlie were kneeling over me, their frightened faces close to mine. Between them, through snow-laden branches, I saw a gray-white sky. Morning.

"Did the snow stop?" I asked.

"Oh, thank God," Mama said. She slid her arm beneath my shoulders and gently sat me up.

I was alone in the buffalo-robe bed. The snow had created a thick blanket during the night. Women were digging frantically through *drifts, looking for buried supplies. Men were prodding our spent oxen with sticks, forcing them to stand.*

Everyone was moving in slow motion. Except for the distant sound of a woman weeping, the scene was eerily silent.

Mama hovered closer. "It took a long time to wake you," she said softly. She rubbed my arm as though to thaw me out.

Something inside me began to sink.

"Is everyone getting ready to go through the pass?"

Mama dropped her hand. She turned her head away.

"Charlie?" I said.

The answer was already in his face.

"No, Puss." His voice cracked. "The pass is closed. We're trapped."

ONE

APRIL 1846. HOME.

I frowned into the mirror above my empty dresser. "This dress is so plain." I squirmed beneath the taut linen fabric. "And stiff!"

The blue plaid cloth hung from a crisp white collar to the middle of my calves and was loosely cinched at the waist. No more scoop-necked, short-sleeved city dresses for me. Mama said they'd be ruined on the trail and had donated them all to the Methodist Church. Everything else we owned was given away, packed in the wagons out front or, like our bedroom furniture, left behind for the people who bought our house.

Eight-year-old Patty watched me from her stripped bed, porcelain doll in her lap. My parents' voices and the clatter of chains rode the early morning chill through our window. A horse whinnied.

I frowned into the mirror again, then turned to Patty. "Why do you think Mama made our pockets so deep? I can stick my whole arm down one. And these." I held up a pair of ugly, round-toed ankle boots. "Does she think we're going to *walk* all the way to California?"

Patty looked down and fumbled with the hem of her doll's silk dress. "Are you scared, Puss?" she asked.

"Scared?" I tugged irritably at my sleeves. "Not at all."

"Well, I am."

Patty scared? Since when? She and our three-year-old brother Tommy had been eager to go pioneering.

I walked across the room and crouched to look into Patty's dark eyes. Watchful, serious. "An old soul," our Grandma Keyes called her. "Scared of Indians?" I asked. Grandma had pioneered through Kentucky when she was little, and she'd enjoyed scaring Patty and me with stories of tomahawks, painted faces, and kidnapped children for as long as we could remember.

"The Plains Indians aren't like Grandma's Indians," I went on, echoing Grandma's words. "Grandma says they'll want to trade baskets for buttons and glass beads, things like that."

Patty shook her head. "I'm not scared of Injuns."

I thought for a moment. "Because of what those stupid boys at school said about wolves and grizzly bears?"

She bit her lower lip and nodded. I gave her a quick hug and stood up.

"You've no reason to be scared, Patty," I said, returning to the dresser. "Pa would never let anything bad happen to us."

Pa had been itching to go West for more than a year, ever since reading pioneer letters in our Springfield newspaper, the *Sangamon Journal*. After that, he bought a newly published, yellow-covered book called *The Emigrants' Guide to Oregon and California*, written by a man named Lansford Hastings. Hastings' glowing descriptions of fertile valleys and year-round sunshine convinced Pa to sell his business and herd the whole family across the frontier. It didn't matter whether or not we wanted to go. Pa wanted to go, and Pa always got his way.

Despite the odd costume, I *did* want to go. I was twelve, going on thirteen, and I'd never been outside the state of Illinois. Besides, Pa had promised I could ride my pony Billy alongside him. Every day. All two thousand miles.

Yesterday I'd said good-bye to schoolmates I'd known nearly my whole life. And last night our parlor was filled with friends and relatives: Uncle Jim, scowling in disapproval; Aunt Lydia, sad-faced but resigned; and Mary, who was not only my cousin, but also my very best friend.

"You'll write me a letter from the trail, won't you?" she asked me through watery blue eyes.

I fought the lump rising in my throat. Mary and I had shed more than enough tears about our separation these last months.

"I'll try," I said. "But—"

Mary leaned in close. "I don't care if you can't spell, Puss. Write anyway. *Promise*."

I felt the color rise to my cheeks. "All right, I promise. But don't show my letter to anyone at school. Especially Mrs. Roark."

Patty pushed herself off the bed, her new boots thumping the floor and jolting me to the present. "I'm going to see if Grandma's ready," she said, heading out the door. Her footsteps echoed down the hall.

I pulled my hair behind my ears and began braiding. Wolves. Bears. *Indians*. My heart sped up. Safety in numbers, I reminded myself. Pa said we'd be traveling in the company of a family named Donner.

I poked around my shell jewelry case for a hairpin and fixed my braid into a knot. Then something caught my eye. A pink and white strand lay beneath the jumble of hairpins. My rosary necklace! I lifted it out and ran a thumb and forefinger down the delicate beads. I studied the tiny image on its silver crucifix.

How long since I'd hidden it there? Two years at least. I glanced out the door into the empty hallway. Pushing back a twinge of guilt, I dropped the necklace into the deep pocket of my dress, then clasped the shell case shut.

A few minutes later I was standing out front, holding Mama's black and brown terrier, Cash. The wide dirt road in front of our house was filled with canvas-covered wagons, grownups hailing one another, and scores of confused livestock milling about.

George and Jacob Donner were in their sixties—too old for such a difficult journey, Uncle Jim had declared more than once. But the gray-haired brothers were lively and cheerful as they helped Pa hitch his new black and white oxen—two to a yoke—to the wooden tongue jutting from the front of our family wagon.

I knew I shouldn't be prideful, but it was hard not to be proud of that wagon. Like most others, our family wagon was about fourteen feet long, but that's where the likeness ended. Pa had designed it to be half again as high as any other, needing six oxen to pull it, instead of the usual four. Long boards spanned the wheels along each side, widening the wagon by several feet and allowing for second-story platforms with built-in beds. The entrance was on one side, so instead of climbing in through the front or back, we could step up a folding staircase into a little parlor with facing spring sofas, the high-backed velvet kind found in stagecoaches. Pa had even installed a small wood-burning stove. Its pipe poked through the high canvas roof.

Cash wriggled out of my arms when the Donner children poured from their wagons. There were so many! Most were little, but a girl about my height with a long, dark braid walked out from behind the last wagon, straightened her skirt, and looked around. Then she walked toward me, smiling.

"Are you Virginia?" Her eyes were a startling turquoise. "I'm Leanna Donner." She gestured toward several little girls who were crouching down to pet Cash. "Those are my sisters."

Mama had said I'd make new friends. No one could ever take Mary's place, of course, but this girl seemed nice enough. "Yes, my friends call me Puss—"

"Oh! I already know all about you," Leanna broke in. "My ma says you have your own pony. And that your family is Methodist like us. And that you go to a big school here in the city." She wound her braid around her fingers. "Ours is—was—just a one-room schoolhouse. Not fancy like yours, but I'm going to miss it."

I'm sure I blinked. "You like school?"

"Of course. Don't you?"

"Not all of it," I admitted. "Anyway, my Uncle Jim says there are no schools where we're going. California isn't even part of the United States, you know."

Leanna tugged at my sleeve. "Come see what we brought."

I followed her inside a wagon that smelled of new pine and coffee beans. A wood box filled with books was wedged between two sacks of flour. I sat on a stack of folded blankets while Leanna riffled through it.

"Ma's a teacher," she said, holding out a math book. "She's going to start up a school for all of us soon as we get there."

"Hmm." I thumbed through pages of times tables, trying to look interested. Why did a schoolteacher have to be coming with us? My face grew warm as I recalled Mrs. Roark's parting words in the schoolyard. "God speed, dear." Then she'd handed me a small primer. "This is to help with your spelling. Keep working."

I hoped Leanna wouldn't notice my flushed cheeks. "I think Mama might need my help with something," I said.

"All right, Virginia. I mean Puss." She flashed me another smile. "I'm supposed to be watching my little sisters, anyway."

I walked toward our family wagon through a whirl of activity. The Donner brothers and some other men were lining up livestock behind the wagon train. Several dogs, including Cash, barked as they chased each other around the wagons' spoked wheels. The sun was burning off the morning's chill and the sky, overcast earlier, was beginning to clear. As I made my way forward, I saw Tommy and several little Donner boys running from wagon to wagon, whooping and stirring up clouds of dirt. Pa had disappeared, but up ahead his black mare, Glaucus, tossed her head and danced in place as though she knew she'd be leading the train. Even Billy, tied to the back of our kitchen wagon, stomped impatiently. I paused to calm him.

"Hey, Billy," I said, stroking his muzzle. "Just a bit longer. Soon you and I will be racing far ahead of everyone here."

I glanced into the kitchen wagon. Mama and I had reorganized it a dozen times with things we'd need on the frontier: a camp stove, canvas bags stuffed with metal dishes and utensils, a butter churn, flour, grains, coffee beans, cornmeal, sugar and salt, an extra saddle and bridle, Pa's guns and ammunition, and three folding tents. Our third wagon, the one Pa called the supply wagon, held things we'd need once we got to California: Mama's good china, oil lamps, table and bed linens, family heirlooms, Pa's best books, and a few children's books, too. The supply wagon also held sacks of seed and farming tools.

Could we be more ready? Pa had thought of everything.

Inside the family wagon Mama somehow looked crisp as always, even in a plain prairie dress like mine. Decked out in white apron and house cap, she introduced me to the Donner brothers' wives. The taller woman had soft gray bangs beneath the rim of her wide bonnet. The shorter woman stood stiff as a ramrod, and her hair was pulled into a tight knot. She was definitely Leanna's mother. She *looked* like a schoolteacher.

"Call her Aunt Betsy and me Aunt Tamsen, dear," the schoolteacher instructed, gesturing toward the gray-banged woman. "That way, we'll always know which Mrs. Donner you're talking to."

"We're going to be one big family for quite a while," Aunt Betsy said. Crinkles appeared at the corners of her eyes when she smiled.

Mama nodded pleasantly as the women admired the mirror Pa had wired between two of the wood bows that supported our canvas roof. But when they left, her shoulders sagged.

"Finish up storing those clothes, will you dear?" she said, untying her apron and removing her cap. "I'm going out to get Tommy." Mama's voice quivered just enough to make me look at her questioningly. She gave me a crooked half smile.

"A difficult morning is all," she explained. "One minute I think I'm ready to go, and the next…"

"I know, Mama. Me too." Still, I was surprised that tears sprang to my eyes.

I was cramming clothing beneath one of the platforms when I heard Grandma's voice outside.

"You be careful now, James Reed!"

I peeked out the door. Pa was carrying my tiny grandma down the porch stairs. She was perched in his arms like a child, specs halfway down her nose, mouth in a tight line. Patty walked alongside them. How alike Patty and Pa looked, with their dark hair and eyes! My real father died when I was a baby. Pa was the only father I'd ever known, and I knew he loved me every bit as much as he did Patty and Tommy. Still, at unexpected moments like this, I felt a pang of envy.

The little procession passed a knot of four or five teamsters who were talking excitedly. Teamsters walked alongside the oxen, calling out commands and cracking long leather whips to make them pull our wagons. In return, they got pay and free meals all the way to California. Milt Elliott stood a head above the others, hat pushed back from his broad forehead, big ears red from the sun. Milt was the foreman at Pa's furniture factory. When Pa sold the factory to go West, Milt signed on as our teamster.

Despite Grandma's fussing, Pa easily maneuvered her into the wagon and gently propped her up against the mound of feather pillows on her platform bed. Then he rushed off to his next task.

"Are you sad too, like Mama?" I asked as Patty and I tucked her in.

Grandma smiled and gave my hand a little squeeze. "I'm pioneering again, dear," she said. "I couldn't be happier."

The wagon lurched forward, then stopped.

"Mercy!" Grandma squeezed harder. "What was that?"

"We're leaving!" Mama, one arm cradling Cash, herded Tommy into the wagon and pulled the stairs up behind her.

My stomach flip-flopped. This was it. We were leaving home. Right this minute. Forever.

Our wagon lurched again. I grabbed a wood bow to steady myself. This time the wheels continued to turn. "Let's go, boys!" I heard Pa yell from somewhere up front.

"Children, come here." Mama lifted the flap at the foot of Grandma's bed for a last look at our house. But Patty and Tommy weren't interested; they scrambled up front to watch Milt drive the oxen. I hovered near the door.

"Pa said I could ride with him," I said.

Mama's eyes were fixed on the house. "Go on ahead, dear."

I jumped down through the door, untied Billy, and stood aside as all nine wagons, followed by a stream of horses and livestock, passed by. Then I was alone, holding Billy's reins and looking back at our house through a cloud of dust. The windows were blank, and the wide porch was empty. It already looked different: shrunken, lifeless.

I closed my eyes and tried to remember the sounds outside my bedroom window—chirping sparrows, rustling maple leaves—but all I could hear was the rattling of departing wagons. I squeezed my eyes tighter, trying to see Mary's face, but Billy tugged at the reins, hurrying my good-bye.

Home wasn't here anymore. Home was rolling down the road. I took a deep breath, mounted Billy, and rode full speed after my father.

TWO

MAY 1846. PA'S FIRST MISTAKE.

"We'll reach Independence within the hour," Pa said. Billy was feeling frisky. He tossed his mane and strained to break into a run. I tightened the reins to pace him with Glaucus who, Pa claimed, had more self-control.

The sun climbed behind us and the sky filled with clear blue light. The trail, etched with parallel wagon tracks, stretched ahead as far as I could see. I inhaled the earthy scent of new grass.

Sometime in the past four weeks my father had taken to wearing a narrow-brim hat pushed back on his head, a jaunty red scarf around his neck, and a hunting knife looped to his belt. Though his coarse beard was carefully trimmed as always, his new look reminded me of the illustrations of pioneers in that yellow-covered book, the one that had convinced him year-round sunshine awaited us in California. All last year, he'd read passages aloud to Mama until he finally got her to change her mind about leaving Springfield.

"Listen to what Lansford Hastings says *here*, Margaret," he said over supper last fall. I paused midbite to look at Mama, and Patty stopped chewing. Only Tommy, studiously using his spoon to remove every pea from his chicken stew, didn't react.

Mama looked up from across the table and slowly shook her head, her looped braids brushing her shoulders. "James, for the last time, I'm not dragging the children across the wilderness to this promised land of yours."

Pa lifted the book from his lap and read anyway.

> "The climate of the Western section is that of perpetual spring, having no excess of heat or of cold. It is the most uniform and delightful."

Then he read the author's claims that disease was almost unknown in California.

"No disease! How can that be true?" But Mama's tone was more hopeful than questioning, and a wave of sorrow washed over me when I realized why. Diphtheria had struck Springfield a year earlier, killing scores of children, including my new baby brother, Gerson. Heartbroken, Mama had worried over the rest of us children ever since.

She laid down her fork and leaned forward. "What else does he say, James?"

"*Kee-eeeee-arr!*" A red-tailed hawk soared overhead, startling me back to the low hills that surrounded us. Billy settled into a rhythmic pace, and Pa and I followed the well-worn trail in comfortable silence.

Mama, I recalled, had told me Independence would be full of travelers going every which way. Surely one of them would carry a letter back to Springfield—and Mary—for me.

What would I write? That pioneering had turned out to be fun—like a long campout with two other families.

That I sometimes sat with Grandma in back of the wagon and waved to pioneers camped by an orchard or cornfield. They would call out, "Bound for California? So are we!"

That we had already traveled two hundred fifty miles, following the half-mile wide Missouri River through farm country, then ferrying across it near a town called Lexington.

I was used to riding western saddle, but not for hours at a time. Rashes appeared on the insides of my legs. Aunt Betsy declared my pantaloons weren't thick enough and gave me a pair of her son Will's trousers. The pant legs fell below the hem of my dress and gathered at my ankles. Will, twelve and bashful, was red-faced when I lifted my skirt to show them off at breakfast, but Pa laughed so hard he nearly choked on his coffee. Mama pursed her lips as though in disapproval, but I caught her smiling as she leaned over the camp stove.

Each day when the sun got high, Mama laid out the patchwork quilt Aunt Lydia had made us, and all three families picnicked together. We called our lunch "nooning," and we enjoyed ourselves so much we sometimes stayed two or three hours. After supper, when the sky grew darker than dark and filled with glowing stars, we gathered around one big campfire to tell stories and sing songs and listen to the grownups talk about our new lives in California.

I'd write Mary that Independence, Missouri, was the westernmost town in the United States, and that Pa had made plans to join forces there with a big group of pioneers called the Russell Company. Plains Indians were friendly, Pa had told me, but they still might try to steal a horse or two if they thought they could get away with it.

The knowledge we were getting closer to Indian Territory made my throat tighten. Grandma had assured me the Plains Indians wouldn't hurt *people*, like the Indians who had stolen her aunt away in Kentucky sixty years earlier. But what if they tried to steal Billy?

Pa's voice broke through my worry. "Those are wagon circles up ahead, Puss. We're almost there."

Independence sat atop a low hill. Clusters of white-topped wagons stood on both sides of the trail, nearly blocking my view. As we drew close, I saw only a few women and children moving about them.

"What did I tell you?" Pa said, grinning widely. "We're going to set up camp right here with the others."

"Where are all the people?" I asked.

"They're most likely in town buying provisions." Pa swung off his saddle and glanced back impatiently at our lagging wagons. "Exchanging information," he continued, more to himself than to me. "Joining forces."

Pa's enthusiasm spread to the others as they caught up and formed a wagon circle. After a quick lunch of beef jerky and dried apples, we discussed who would go into town. I was disappointed when Leanna told me she had to stay in camp to watch her sisters. Tommy wanted to stay behind with the little Donner boys, and Patty wanted to be with Grandma.

"But buy good things to eat," Patty said. "Candy."

Mama sat on the wagon steps with a quill pen and paper, and we children gathered around.

"Is this where we'll get our own ponies, like Puss?" Tommy asked, his hand on Mama's knee.

"No, silly," Patty said. "Pa said not 'til we get to California." She leaned over Mama's shoulder. "Candy," she repeated.

Mama started writing. "You need a bonnet with a wider brim, Puss," she said without looking up. "And riding gloves. Your face is getting brown and your hands are getting freckled."

"I don't need gloves, Mama. I don't need another bonnet, either." How much more covered up could I be? "I need new boots." I stuck out a foot and wiggled it around. "See? Mine are getting tight already."

Mama scanned me from my boots all the way up to my face. "For heaven's sakes, dear. Put on a clean dress before we go into town. You do have two more, you know. And tidy up your hair, too."

The town square reminded me of downtown Springfield on the Fourth of July—so crammed with people, horses, and wagons I could barely make out the storefronts. Mama, Pa, and I stopped to get our bearings near a corral with livestock for sale. Although we'd just nooned at camp, scents of barbecue and spun sugar made my mouth water, and all around I heard the laughter of shoppers, the clanging from a blacksmith shop, and the banging of piano keys from a dance hall. Someone was playing *Jimmy Crack Corn* on a harmonica, and I hummed along with the tune. Pa pointed out a group of Mexican men wearing high-coned, wide-brimmed hats. "Those hats are called *sombreros*," he told me. "You'll see a lot of those in California."

"Look, Puss. Indians." Mama nodded toward a pair of tan-skinned old women with long gray braids. They were standing outside a store, wrapped in faded blankets and staring passively into the distance.

My eyes widened. I knew it was rude to stare, but I couldn't help myself. These were the first real Indians I'd ever seen. Why, they weren't scary at all.

"Patty will be so mad she stayed back in camp with Grandma," I said.

"We'll be here a few days," Mama answered. "You can bring her back tomorrow."

We pushed our way into the crowd outside the general store. Several men were gathered on the corner, shaking hands and talking. Pa left to join them while Mama and I went inside.

I was grudgingly glad Mama had made me wash up and change my dress before walking into town. There must have been a half-dozen girls my age in the dim, high-ceilinged store, some of them wearing white, short-sleeved frocks of delicate fabrics like I'd worn in Springfield. City girls, I thought nostalgically, eyeing their slim button shoes. Others wore long-sleeved prairie dresses and thick boots like my own. I exchanged shy smiles across grain barrels with one such girl, short and blonde like Mary. Maybe this girl was with the Russell Company. I hoped so.

Like the mercantile in Springfield, this store's narrow aisles and high shelves were jammed with clothing and raw fabric, honey and molasses, cooking utensils and dishes, guns and ammunition.

Mama was in a good mood. She bought me lightweight riding gloves and bigger boots, yarn and buttons for herself, a little Mexican sombrero for Tommy, a dark-blue sunbonnet for Patty, and sweet taffy and lemon drops for the whole family.

Our teamster, Milt, was waiting for us outside the store. He wore a silly fur hat with no brim. His already big ears seemed even bigger.

"There's a mountain man over there, Mrs. Reed," he said, pointing down the main road. "He's selling fur hats and hides if you're interested."

I peered through the crowd. A longhaired man dressed from head to toe in animal skins was holding up a hairy robe for those passing by. He had a toothless smile, and his skin looked like cracked leather.

Mama wrinkled her nose and shook her head.

Milt laughed. "Mr. Reed asked if I'd walk you two ladies back to the wagons. He and the Donner brothers are still tracking down Colonel Russell."

Pa and the Donner men returned to camp as we were finishing supper. The sun, a hazy red line on the horizon, cast long shadows across the wagon circle. I pulled a shawl over my shoulders and greeted Pa drowsily as he sat next to Tommy. He pulled off his hat, pushed back his hair, and stared hungrily at the Dutch oven on the camp stove. Mama dished up beef and beans on a metal plate and searched his face as she handed it to him. "Is something wrong, James?"

Pa stared down at his plate a long moment. "I'm afraid I have bad news. Colonel Russell and his company left Independence three days ago."

"They're gone? But James, all this time you've been telling me we'd join up with them here! What happened?"

The alarm in Mama's voice startled me wide-awake. Pa's words had drained her face of color.

I met Patty's widened eyes across the fire. *Mama was scared.* A knot formed in my stomach.

Pa stabbed a forkful of beef. "The agreement was to meet Colonel Russell this week. I thought that meant anytime 'til week's end." He shoved the meat into his mouth and swallowed it whole. "Russell must have meant *first* part of the week."

Mama got quiet whenever upset, and she was very quiet now. She sank down next to Patty and studied her hands. Tommy, unaware of any danger, hummed under his breath as he drew stick figures in the powdery dirt. Voices drifted from across the circle where the Donners were eating.

At our campfire there was only the sound of Pa's fork clicking his plate. The knot in my stomach tightened.

"Are we going to turn around?" I asked, hoping to break the silence. For a moment I envisioned us back in Springfield, unpacking our wagons and reclaiming our house—our adventure over.

Maybe it was for the best. At least we'd be safe.

Pa stirred his food. "Of course not, Puss."

I scooted closer to the flames. "Are we going to wait here for another big company, then?"

"No," he answered, watching Mama. "We're going to catch up with Colonel Russell."

Mama looked up from her hands. "Will it take long?"

"Only a few days." Pa's eyes took us all in. "No more dallying here. We're setting out early tomorrow."

"Oh! But—" Patty said, then bit her lip. She looked as though she might cry. I had told her I'd take her into town to see the Indian women in the morning.

"And no more long noonings," Pa added, setting down his plate. "We have to catch up with the Russell Company before we reach the Great Plains."

I remembered my worries about Plains Indians stealing Billy. Was that just this morning? I remembered Grandma's Indian stories, too, and a queasy feeling passed through me. Would Plains Indians steal *children* if they thought they could get away with it?

Pa pulled Tommy into his lap and abruptly changed the subject. "We're getting a new traveling companion tomorrow. We met him in town. A Chicagoan named Charles Stanton. He lost his business, and he's going to California for a new start."

"Another teamster?" Mama asked. The edge in her tone had softened.

Pa shook his head. "I wouldn't hire him on as a teamster. He's not a big man. He already has his own horse and money, anyway. He just needs someone to travel with."

Then Pa started talking about rumors he'd heard in town—something about the United States and Mexico being on the verge of war. "Things are happening just as I predicted, Margaret," he said, giving Tommy a little squeeze. "California will break away from Mexico sooner than later. Then it will be all ours."

The flames burned low and my parents' voices faded. The tension between them had passed, but that didn't ease my mind. Pa had planned this journey for nearly a year, yet somehow he'd been wrong about our meeting date with Colonel Russell.

I slid a hand into my pocket and felt through the rosary beads until I found the crucifix. I ran my thumb over its raised image.

"We're jumping off tomorrow," Pa said. The morning's excitement was back in his voice. I looked up. Pa was smiling at Tommy, ruffling his hair. "We're jumping off the edge of the world."

THREE

MAY 1846. ON OUR OWN.

I knelt beside a shallow creek, scrubbing breakfast dishes with sand and rinsing them in the frigid current. My fingers felt stiff as icicles.

A harsh honking filled the air. I looked up to see a small flock of geese flapping overhead, a V shape against the gray-white sky. The noise mirrored my mood.

I was still in a stew over Pa's announcement last night. I'd never known my father to be wrong about anything. So how could he have been wrong about such an important meeting? Mama, after her initial alarm, had taken our change of plans in stride. And judging by their cheerful greetings early this morning, so had the Donner grownups.

But I couldn't let it go. As Tommy tossed pebbles into the water and watched Cash run from one splash to another, my mind spun with questions. Could Pa have been wrong about something else too, back when I was too young to realize?

I thought about the rosary beads hidden deep in my pocket.

When I was ten, Pa allowed me to attend a Catholic service with a neighbor girl named Lucy. "This will be a good experience for her," he assured Mama.

I was awestruck from the moment I walked through the carved doors. Hundreds of tiny flames flickered in the dim entryway, and farther on, sunlight poured through stained-glass windows that lined the walls. Life-size statues of saints stood in alcoves beneath each window.

This church didn't have Sunday school like our Methodist Church. Here, children were allowed to sit in pews with the grown-ups. The white-robed priest spoke from a high altar, murmuring foreign words in a singsong lilt. Then the parishioners recited a prayer in English, their voices rising and echoing off the walls.

"I don't know that one," I whispered, watching their upturned faces.

"The Apostle's Creed. Part of the Rosary." Lucy handed me the little silver crucifix she'd been holding. It was attached to a pink-and-white beaded strand. "Keep this. I have others."

I'd never prayed this way before. I fingered the tiny beads and listened intently to the rhythmic voices. Something inside me shifted, and a sense of peace enveloped me like a weightless cloak.

That afternoon at supper I told my parents I wanted to go back. "I like it there," I said. "I want to be a Catholic."

Mama and Pa exchanged amused smiles. "We're Methodists, dear," Mama said.

"I know. But I like it *better* there."

Pa dabbed at his beard with a napkin, then laid it back on his lap. "Of course you like it better there. The Catholics have a very pretty building. But religion is more than pretty buildings and medieval rituals."

My cheeks began to burn. How could I explain that Methodist Sunday school, with its familiar friends and recited verses, left me feeling empty?

"I didn't mean that, Pa. I meant I felt closer to God there."

Patty looked up from her plate. Mama turned from me to Pa and back to me. "Oh, Puss. What a thing to say."

Pa wasn't smiling anymore. "You were not closer to God there, Puss. Quite the contrary." His tone was level, controlled. "You simply let yourself get swept away."

I knew that tone well. It meant our conversation was over. But what was Pa telling me? That God liked Methodists better than Catholics?

I never went back to the Catholic Church. I buried the rosary necklace under the hairpins in my shell case. As the months passed, the experience faded.

Until the morning we left Springfield.

I shook water off a rinsed cup and pushed the troublesome memory aside. Voices drifted downstream from camp—Milt's steady drone, Pa's quick laugh, Uncle Jake's high-pitched scolding as he yoked the oxen. The trickling waters muffled their words, but Uncle George's gravelly voice joined in, followed by a voice I hadn't heard before—warm and genial.

Must be the new man Pa told us about last night, I thought, stacking rinsed dishes in the canvas bag. Hopefully he'd be nice, like Uncle George and Uncle Jake.

Tommy dawdled on the way back to camp, hoping to find a snake or lizard for Cash. By the time we got there most of the men had left to gather up the livestock. Only a stranger—a short, clean-shaven man with a narrow-brimmed hat—stood by the family wagon with Mama, Aunt Tamsen, and several small Donner boys and girls. One of his hands gripped a satchel; the other, the reins of a sorrel horse. Quilt-wrapped parcels were strapped to his horse's back.

"We share an interest in plant life, Mr. Stanton," Aunt Tamsen was saying. The schoolteacher smiled, her hands on one of Leanna's little sister's shoulders. "I'd be happy to lend you my book on botany."

Mama drew me next to her. She smiled, too. Why, this man had won the women over within minutes. "Meet Virginia, Mr. Stanton," she said, smoothing my hair in an irritating way. "She's our eldest."

"Miss Reed." Mr. Stanton peered at me through rimless glasses that magnified friendly brown eyes. He smiled as though he already knew me. "Your father tells me you're quite a rider. Maybe you'll allow Banjo and me to join you now and then."

Mr. Stanton looked old—at least twenty—yet his friendly manner put me at ease. I noticed Banjo's shiny coat and brushed mane. Mr. Stanton must love horses, too.

"Have you seen my pa's mare yet?" Surprised by my own boldness, I handed the bag of washed dishes to Mama. "Her name's Glaucus. She's a real racehorse. I'll show her to you. I'll show you Billy, too. He's *my* pony."

Later that morning Mr. Stanton joined Pa and me as we rode on ahead of the wagons. The men talked about Mexican war rumors, but I barely listened. I kept looking over my shoulder as the rooftops of Independence disappeared from view. There would be no other town until we reached California, four whole months from now.

"Good-bye, United States of America," I called out. Mr. Stanton turned in his saddle and smiled. "The United States will follow us all the way to the Pacific, Virginia. We're just leading the way."

That was all it took for Pa to start in about how California would surely be the next state in the Union, and he and Mr. Stanton resumed their conversation. I had heard Pa talk on this uninteresting subject many times, and I dropped farther back on the trail.

Independence was behind us, and I hadn't had a chance to write to Mary as I'd promised. We'd been passing people going the opposite direction nearly every day since we left home—lone riders and groups of two or three men, mostly—but who knew when one of them would be willing to carry a letter all the way back to Springfield? A man on horseback might cover at least three times the distance each day than a wagon train, but it could still take days, weeks even. I sighed and stroked Billy's neck. I'd already forgotten some of the things I planned to tell her.

A cool flutter lifted the brim of my bonnet. Far to my left, swelling clouds darkened the sky. I bent my head against a gathering wind and focused on the gray topknot between Billy's ears.

The wind fell, rose, and fell again. I followed Pa and Mr. Stanton over gentle hills marked by greening cottonwood trees. Here and there I noticed scatterings of trembling wildflowers—spiky lupine and pale poppies.

My mind drifted back to the winter months before we left Springfield. Pa had shown Patty and me maps of our route—first, the Oregon Trail, which we joined this morning when we left Independence, and then the California Trail, which would lead us over the Sierra Nevada Mountains into California. He described high, grassy plains that stretched as far as the eye could see in every direction and showed us sketches of odd stone formations with names like Courthouse Rock and Scotts Bluff. He said we'd cross sandy deserts and climb mountains so steep, it might take a fourth yoke of oxen to pull our family wagon uphill.

I had never seen a mountain. I raised my head, trying to imagine how high a mountain might be, but the roiling clouds reclaimed my attention in time to see a shimmery veil cascade to the earth.

I gripped the reins. "It's raining over there!" I called out. Light flickered on the horizon.

Pa and Mr. Stanton reined in their horses and waited for me to catch up. We heard a faraway roll of thunder.

"Nothing to be afraid of, Puss," Pa declared. "That storm is miles south of us and moving straight east."

I glanced at Mr. Stanton. He didn't look as sure, but after a moment he nodded in agreement.

Billy trembled beneath me.

FOUR

MAY 1846. SPRING STORMS.

I woke to the darkness of early morning and a light rain pattering the canvas roof. We'd been trapped in our family wagon for four days and nights. I lay beside Patty and Tommy, imagining how I'd describe this assault of spring storms to Mary. I'd have to remember the important things: How the trail turned to thick, gooey mud that made it impossible to go farther. How hail hammered the canvas like buckshot. How water leaked through the seams and got Grandma's bed wet. And how lightning lit up the inside of our wagon and made us all jump, even Pa, as he fed sticks into the wood-burning stove.

We were, he reminded us often, the only family with a stove inside our wagon to keep us warm. I felt bad for Leanna, huddled in her parents' smaller family wagon with four sisters. And that nice Mr. Stanton, alone in his tent, probably shivering and miserable.

In between downpours most everyone left their wagons to cook over camp stoves, tend to the animals, and check on one another. But the grownups' worried conversations around soggy campfires raised frightening questions. Was the Russell

Company managing to move ahead while our wagons continued to sink in the mud? How would we catch up with them
now?

Between Springfield and Independence, we passed pioneer
families who'd turned back and were heading home for one
reason or another. Now Mama and Grandma, fearing we'd lost
the Russell Company for good, talked about turning back too.
Pa would have none of it. "Too late," he finally stated one night
as the wind wailed outside. "There's nothing to go back to.
We've sold everything."

Yet the possibility we might turn back—however brief—
steered my thoughts to Springfield and Mary.

If we had storms like these back home, I thought, we'd have
our big house to protect us. Mary would come over every day
and we'd play hide and seek upstairs or checkers in the parlor
or sip hot chocolate in front of the fireplace.

I sighed and tried to remember Pa's reasons for picking up
and moving. Free land, he'd said. Healthy climate. Prosperity.

Many of Pa's friends back home had disapproved of the move.

"But you're already prosperous, James!" Reverend Filbert blus-
tered on the church steps when Pa told him the news. He glanced
down at me, eyes wide, then back at Pa. "Why risk everything for
the unknown? You've worked so hard for what you have."

But just as many had encouraged him to go.

"I wish I had your guts, Reed," said Mr. Bennett, at the
bank. "There's a new world waiting out West." He winked at
me. "What an adventure you're going to have, little lady!"

And that, I was sure, was Pa's real reason for herding us all
to California: the irresistible adventure of it all.

Now the wind picked up and began to howl. I wanted to
hold my rosary, but my dress hung from a nail on a nearby

wood bow. I didn't dare get up and take the necklace from my pocket. What would Mama say if she knew I was carrying it with me?

Patty stirred beside me. She sat up and tried to shake Tommy awake, with no luck. "Will you read me that book about Daniel Boone again, Puss?" she asked. Cash, who slept at our feet, lifted his head groggily, then laid it back down.

I inhaled the wagon's dank, metallic smell. "Too dark, Patty. I'll think up a story instead."

Outside, the rain continued to fall.

By the time the weeklong storms moved on, our family wagon had sunk all the way to its axles. Everyone except Grandma climbed out while Milt and Pa yoked extra oxen to pull it free. The Donners' teamsters, grumbling about our wagon's size and weight, lifted and pushed from behind. Patty and I held hands in a soggy meadow as we watched. We knew Grandma was being jostled in her bed.

That night the pitch-black sky displayed a mass of glittering stars. Most everyone, even the smallest children, stayed up late at campfire to warm ourselves and spend our first night together in a week. Dried mud was caked on boots and clothing, but there was no time to do a wash—"Not until we catch up with Russell," Pa said—so we scraped off what we could.

Aunt Tamsen talked about groups of stars called constellations. I huddled in a blanket with Leanna, counting each star in the Little Dipper's tail until I reached the brightest, the North Star.

Now and then I glanced across the fire at my parents. They were sitting close together, exchanging worried whispers. Grandma had been coughing all afternoon. She was finally asleep in the wagon, with Patty keeping watch at her side.

Mr. Stanton picked up a small branch and tossed it into the flames. The wood sizzled and gave off a damp, bitter smell. "I daresay that's the first time any of us weathered a storm with so little shelter," he said. The firelight glinted off his glasses as he packed his pipe. I leaned forward. Anything Mr. Stanton had to say was probably important. "I expect we'll experience a lot more firsts on our way to California," he added.

I knew what he meant. Our journey from Springfield to Independence wasn't pioneering; it was practice. We'd been traveling through our own civilized country, and help was always nearby. But here on the frontier, no matter what happened, we were truly on our own.

"I, for one, feel quite safe," Aunt Tamsen said. She sat between Aunt Betsy and Uncle George, shawl around her shoulders, arms hugging her knees. "They say there are hundreds of wagons on the Oregon Trail this summer. Why, that's thousands of pioneers! We're like one long ribbon stretching all the way to the Pacific."

Muffled coughing drifted from our family wagon. Mama and Pa rose to check on Grandma. I remained at the fire, but my shoulders tensed.

"Nearly every day someone passes us," Aunt Tamsen continued, pulling her shawl closer. "Or we meet someone heading east, like those two trappers this morning—the ones who told us Colonel Russell was stuck in the mud all week, same as us, and is only a day or so ahead, across the next river."

"That's true, my dear," Uncle George said. Firelight illuminated the bushy gray eyebrows below his black hat. "But they also told us about those two little boys who drowned in that river yesterday. Right now it's dangerously high."

A jolt went through me. What? No one had told me two little boys ahead of us drowned!

Uncle Jake stood nearby, hands on his hips, face drawn. Even his graying mustache drooped these days. He'd become sickly soon after leaving Springfield, and the rainstorms had left him even frailer. "Brothers, they were," he sighed. "I'll breathe easier when we're all on the other side."

My stomach quivered and I took a long breath to calm it. I'd never learned to swim. None of us children had.

I fixed my eyes on the North Star, then lowered them to the horizon, where the Kansas River waited, swollen from rain.

FIVE

MAY 1846. UNCHARTED WATERS.

I heard the river before I saw it. Its current sounded like a windstorm roaring through a thousand trees. Closer, I was relieved to see the Kansas, at two hundred yards across, wasn't nearly as wide as the Missouri. But it was high and swift, with branches and other debris swirling through its dark waters.

Pa and I dismounted and waited for the others to catch up. The early afternoon sky was clear, but the rains had left their mark on the flooded banks. Twisted branches littered the ground, and on the other side of the river an oak tree had been sliced in two by a lightning bolt.

"We have to cross today," Pa said. "We can't let the Russell Company get farther ahead than they already are."

I nodded, but my eyes followed what looked like part of a wagon wheel as it traveled downriver. Where were the bodies of the two little brothers? Had they been recovered and buried? Or were they still in the river somewhere?

"I don't see the ferries, Pa. Are we in the right place?"

Pa stroked Glaucus's sleek neck. "Upriver, according to the trappers that came through yesterday. The Caws make a fair amount of money poling river traffic, they said."

"The Caws?"

"We're in Caw country, Puss. They run the ferry boats here."

Indians were going to float us across this river? What was Pa thinking? I started to speak, but stopped myself. It wasn't my place to question him. Maybe Uncle George or Uncle Jake would set him straight. Maybe one of them knew another way to get across.

But as soon as everyone caught up, we traveled upriver to the flat ferry landing where two tethered rafts bobbed near shore. Ten or twelve Caw boatmen with long hair and straw hats waited. Like the women in Independence, these men bore no resemblance to the Indians Grandma described in her stories. They wore white men's clothing, and at least one of them, the one bargaining with Pa, spoke clear English.

I watched with Patty and Tommy from shore as the boatmen easily half rolled and half lifted Uncle George's family wagon onto the first raft. Aunt Tamsen and her daughters, including Leanna, boarded and disappeared inside the wagon. Uncle George stood next to it, a watchman guarding his family. Mr. Stanton was beside him, his narrow-brimmed hat pushed flat on his head.

Patty and Tommy chatted excitedly as we watched four boatmen use long poles to push the heavily loaded raft from shore. I nodded along with their conversation, determined to hide my fear. But the river swirled so! As the Caws pushed farther out, water splashed onto the planks, and I gasped out loud when Mr. Stanton gripped a wheel to steady himself.

Stroke by stroke, the boatmen thrust their poles into the river bottom and guided the raft through the current. How on earth did they keep their balance on the wet surface?

Only twenty minutes after boarding, Leanna and her family disembarked and waved to us from the other side. I waved back, but my eyes were on Mr. Stanton as he helped the Caws push the wagon off the raft.

Pa and Mama joined us as a second raft bearing Uncle George's two supply wagons neared the far shore. "We're next, children," Mama said, and I felt my insides cave.

"Look, Pa!" Patty yelled.

Uncle George's second raft slowly turned in the current, then tipped downriver. We watched transfixed as the wagon nearest its edge began to slide toward the water. A cry escaped Mama, and Pa swore out loud. "How in hell can a wagon that heavy slide sideways? It's packed full with farm equipment!"

The river was shallow near shore, so the Caws on that side were able to wade in to their waists and right the raft while the boatmen frantically poled. Uncle George's wagons were saved, but the whole scene left me shaken.

Tommy's question mirrored my thoughts. "What if that happens to *us*, Pa?"

"It won't." Pa said it so matter-of-factly that not even Mama questioned him.

The Caws had no trouble loading our two supply wagons onto one raft, but loading the family wagon was another matter. Grandma, despite her worsening cough, sat up in her bed, determined to experience every moment of the crossing. The Caws lifted and pushed, but our oversized wagon tilted unsteadily. Pa swore again. I cried out. And Mama, stone-faced, stood with her hand to her throat until the wagon was stable.

By the time we stepped onto the raft's slippery planks, smoke was rising from the Donner campfires on the other side. Mama and Patty entered the wagon and settled themselves next to Grandma. Pa hurried Tommy and me through the door, then handed little Cash in to Tommy. "I'll see you on the other side, son."

Tommy's face fell. "Aren't you coming with us?"

"Pa," I whispered frantically, "Who's going to ride across with us? Where's Milt?"

"Puss, you're safe as can be," Pa answered impatiently. "These men know what they're doing. Just sit still and keep hold of Tommy. Milt and I have to swim the livestock over."

Then he was gone.

I huddled with Tommy on one of the spring sofas as two Caw boatmen on our side of the raft pushed off from shore. The current immediately tried to drag us downriver, and I clutched Tommy's hand.

One gray-haired boatman noticed Tommy and me watching through the door and wiggled his dark eyebrows with each thrust of his pole, sending Tommy into cycles of laughter. I tried to join in, but the forced hilarity caught in my throat. What if we slid off the raft right here? Even if we *could* swim, both shores were now too far away to reach.

I couldn't see Pa and the teamsters swimming the livestock over from inside the wagon, and my imagination spun with dark thoughts. I had watched boatmen swim livestock across the Missouri, but that was their job—they did it every day. Could Pa and Milt and the Donner teamsters control all our animals the way those men did? Would Billy be all right?

And what if Pa fell off Glaucus? This river would certainly carry him away. As the water's roar filled my head, I squeezed Tommy's hand, felt for my rosary with my other hand, shut my eyes, and whispered the Lord's Prayer over and over again. If my family could survive this crossing, we could survive anything.

Tommy's hand slid out of mine. My eyes flew open in time to see Cash darting to the back of the wagon and my little brother climbing out the door toward the eyebrow-wiggling boatman. I stood and yelled, "Tommy, no!" but he jumped down onto the slippery planks. The expression on the old Caw's face mirrored my terror. I heard Mama scream as I bolted out the door.

Tommy slipped on the raft's slick surface the moment he landed. He struggled to stand. "Stay *down*, Tommy!" I yelled. But my feet slid out from under me too, and I sat down with a hard thud.

Tommy shrieked, and I watched helplessly as he began to slide toward the raft's edge.

The Caw motioned for me to be still. He crouched near Tommy and laid down his pole. The raft began to turn in the current.

He scooped Tommy under the arms and in one swift motion stood and handed him through the wagon door to Mama. Seconds later I was dangling in the air like a ragdoll, being lifted back-first through the door as well. The boatman hurriedly retrieved his pole as Mama pulled me farther in.

She wrapped me in trembling arms. "Oh, Puss! Are you all right?"

I nodded numbly.

"They're both inside now, Grandma," I heard Patty report.

"Thank the good Lord," Grandma said. Then she started coughing.

The whole episode took place within a minute. The Caw, looking downward, polled in double time to help right the raft. If it weren't for Tommy's loud wailing and my own pounding heart, I would have wondered if the incident had happened at all.

"Hush now, Tommy," Mama said. "You're not hurt." She pulled Tommy and me back onto the sofa and sat between us, her arms around both our bodies. Silent tears ran down my cheeks. I could still feel the other arms, the surprisingly strong ones that had lifted me back into the wagon.

They had been trembling, too.

The old boatman didn't look at Tommy and me after that. He turned his back as he poled, but I could still see his terror in my mind's eye, and I found myself wondering if he'd witnessed the drowning of those boys two days ago.

Back home in Springfield, my family would have talked about a frightening incident like this for days. But we'd barely stepped onto shore when our attention was sidetracked. There was too much to do: push the wagons off the rafts, pull them up the low bank, set up camp. Pa, Milt, and the Donner teamsters arrived from downriver with scores of exhausted livestock, and they had to be tended to as well.

Pa checked on us as we set up camp. Mama burst into tears when he arrived, and Tommy could hardly wait to tell him what had happened. Pa, still wet from head to toe, crouched down and let him talk, then held him tight.

He looked up. "And you, Puss. You're all right?"

My eyes stung with new tears. "I'm sorry I let Tommy go, Pa. I was praying and then—"

"Don't apologize, Puss." He stood and placed a hand on my shoulder. "I'm just grateful you're both safe. And your grandmother—how did she do?"

Inside the family wagon Grandma's skin was burning hot, but she was sitting up, and her eyes glowed with excitement. "We had a close call, James. Did you see?" Then she told Pa her version of our mishap. "Our girl was quite the heroine, James," she finished, patting my hand. "She saved the day."

"Oh, Grandma," I said. "That's not what happened at all." I turned to Pa. "It was the Caw boatman who saved us."

"All the same," Grandma insisted. "This is one pioneer story you'll be telling *your* grandchildren one day, Puss."

I left Pa and Grandma and wandered back to shore. The rafts were arriving again, this time carrying Uncle Jacob's wagons. That poor old Indian, I thought. Maybe he thinks it was his fault Tommy jumped onto the planks.

I waited for the rafts to land, getting up my nerve to approach the Caw and thank him for saving us. But he wasn't among the boatmen this time.

Within another hour camp was back to normal: Tommy played with the little Donner boys, Patty sat in the wagon tending to Grandma, and Mama lit up the camp stove. Pa and some of the other men stood near the campfire, still drying off and discussing the next day's plan.

I got Billy's brush from the supply wagon, hoping to clean him up before supper. I found him tied to a tree outside the circle, already dry and groomed. Mr. Stanton stood nearby, brushing Glaucus's glossy coat. He glanced over his shoulder.

"Your horses had a rough time of it out there," he said. "I thought I'd clean them up a bit. You and your father surely have other things to do."

"Oh. Why, thank you, Mr. Stanton." My face went hot and I bit my lip. How stiff I sounded! Where had this sudden awkwardness come from? "I guess I could help Mama with supper."

But I didn't want to help Mama with supper. I wanted to stay right here. The sun was setting, and the western sky was streaked with shades of pink and gold. Billy nudged me affectionately. I scratched behind his ears and listened to Mr. Stanton hum as he worked. I recognized the song, a sad one about two children who are left behind.

> And when it came night
> So sad was their plight
> The sun went down
> And the moon gave no light.
> They sobbed and they sighed
> And they bitterly cried

Those two little babes
They lay down and died.

A shiver passed through me and I heard myself blurt out, "I was scared out there. Were you?"

Mr. Stanton stopped brushing and faced me, his expression serious. "I certainly was," he said, tucking the brush handle into his belt. "It's *all* scary, crossing two thousand miles of wilderness to find a new home." He pulled down his brim, shading his glasses. "But you strike me as a brave sort of girl, the way you ride that pony of yours."

Brave? I'd been scared of one thing after another ever since we left Springfield. But my face warmed from the compliment.

"I've been riding my whole life, you know."

"Is that right?"

"Yes. The boys at school, they tease me about being a tomboy. But I'm *not*." I paused. "It's just that I can ride so much faster than any of them. Even sidesaddle."

Oh, that sounded like bragging. Would Mr. Stanton think I was too proud?

But he smiled and nodded toward the river. "And I heard how you tried to save your brother out there. Pioneering may be a scary business, but I'm pretty sure you can handle any challenge that comes your way."

I smiled back, flooded with pleasure. I tossed my brush into the air and caught it. "Today was probably the worst of it, anyway."

"Perhaps," he said, turning back to his work.

"I'll help." I walked to Glaucus's other side and brushed as I hummed along with Mr. Stanton.

The next afternoon clouds of white canvas rose on the horizon. I reined Billy to a halt and stood up in my stirrups.

"Look at all the wagons!"

"Finally." Pa sounded winded, as though he just climbed a mountain on foot. I gave him a curious glance. The air was clear and cold, yet Pa was wiping his brow with his sleeve.

How determined he had been to catch up with the Russell Company, even if it meant bouncing Grandma around. Why, Pa must have been scared all along—really scared—ever since we missed joining up with Colonel Russell back in Independence.

I pushed the unsettling thought aside and tried to concentrate on the sounds ahead. Even at this distance, I could hear children calling, cattle lowing, metal clanging—the same sounds we made whenever we set up camp, magnified a dozen times. There was music mixed in, too.

"Pa, is someone up there fiddling?"

"Sounds like it." He wiped his brow again. "Best we wait here for the others, Puss. We can all ride in together."

Colonel Russell was a stout man with an authoritative air and a Kentucky accent. He accepted us right away, and the company of three hundred pioneers and seventy-two wagons swallowed up our little party of thirty pioneers and nine wagons. At night there were several wagon circles, each one so big that dozens of campfires burned in its center.

The Russell Company had a schedule that took some getting used to. A trumpet blast jolted everyone awake each dawn. Women and girls hurried through breakfast chores, prepared lunches for nooning, tended to little children, and packed wagons for travel, all within an hour or two. I barely had time to dip the dishes into the river we were now following—the Big Blue—and shake them off before dropping them into their canvas bag. Men and boys hurried, too—folding and storing tents, gathering livestock, yoking teams of oxen, and lining up wagons.

Hundreds of oxen hooves and turning wheels created swirling dust clouds, and the farther back in the train a family was, the more dirt it had to deal with. To keep things fair, lineup changed each morning, and the family that led the day before dropped to the back of the caravan. Day by day, each family worked its way forward.

As newcomers, our three families started in back, behind a family named Breen. The Breens were from Ireland, like Pa, but they weren't dark like he was. Mr. and Mrs. Breen both had red hair and freckles, and so did their children—six loud boys and a baby girl. They didn't talk like Pa either. They had an accent—Pa called it an "Irish brogue."

Ed Breen, a rowdy boy my age with a gap-toothed smile, had his own horse, Brownie. He and I sometimes rode a mile or so ahead of the others, then raced back to the wagon train. Sometimes he'd pull ahead, the tail of his raccoon cap flopping against his shaggy red hair. I let him win just often enough to keep him racing me.

Mrs. Breen, a stout, talkative woman with an untidy bun, often slipped into our wagon to sit on our spring sofas and do needlework while the company rattled down the trail. "Ah, what lovely lassies ye have, Margaret!" she said whenever Patty or I stepped in.

Even Pa took to the Breens.

"Patrick Breen certainly does play a lively fiddle," he said one night as we made our way back from campfire. There was no moonlight, and the glow from Pa's lantern cast our shapes across the canvas walls. "Such a nice family. Too bad they are Catholic."

I stopped in my tracks. "There's nothing wrong with being a Catholic, Pa." The force of my emotion caught me off guard. I'd never spoken to him in that tone, and I braced myself for his reaction.

He stopped, too, as if taken aback. I couldn't make out his expression in the dark. He put his arm around my shoulders and started me walking again. "Of course there's not, Puss," he said after a while. "Not if you're raised as one. Not if you don't know any better."

Mama and Tommy had dropped back. "Pa," I said, clearing my throat. "I might want to become a Catholic when we get to California."

How many footsteps until he answered? It must have been a hundred. Then he said, "No daughter of mine will ever be a Catholic." His tone was controlled, but I could hear the anger in it. "Don't bring up this nonsense again."

What did he mean? That he'd stop being my father if I became a Catholic? Tears filled my eyes, and I felt my chin quiver.

"I won't bring it up again, Pa," I said, my voice strangely hoarse. "I promise."

Six

MAY 1846. ALCOVE SPRING.

T he Big Blue River was as almost as high as the Kansas, and there was no one, not even the Caws, to ferry us over. Pa was already one of Colonel Russell's inner circle, and he, Colonel Russell, and some of the other men decided to build one raft big enough to carry up to three wagons at a time.

Milt and Mr. Stanton joined a group of young men to work on the raft. Others, like Pa and the Donner brothers, strengthened wagon axles and tightened wheels that had loosened on the trail.

Mama said she didn't mind stopping for three or four days so that Grandma could get a good rest. Besides, she added, we couldn't have got stranded in a prettier spot.

It *was* pretty. I don't think I'd ever seen so many shades of green in one place before. Hundreds of cottonwoods and maples, leafing out with new growth, wandered from the river-bank to grassy clearings and beyond. In a nearby meadow, clear waters bubbled up from the ground and merged into a water-fall that fell from a rounded ledge. Pa named the area Alcove Spring and carved his initials on the ledge's granite surface.

The break gave us time to wash mud-caked clothes. Mama wanted to be with Grandma every minute, so Patty and I joined the women on shore to scrub and squeeze filthy shirts and dresses in the river flow. We lugged bags of water-soaked petticoats and britches up the banks, then hung long strands of rope between our supply wagons. Our clothes dripped dry in the sun.

I cooked cornmeal johnnycakes on a flat skillet each morning while Mama sat by Grandma's bed, reading Bible passages aloud. Patty stroked Grandma's hair and fed her teaspoons of honey to stifle her cough. After washing the breakfast dishes, I took over for Mama and Patty awhile, telling Grandma about the activities outside until she nodded off.

One morning as I held my hand against her fevered forehead, a niggling thought in the back of my mind caught hold. Grandma had been frail as long as I could remember, but she'd never had a cold this bad. Or this long.

"Mama," I asked when she returned with Patty, "when is Grandma going to start feeling better?"

"Soon, dear," she said. But she lowered her eyes and looked away.

Later that day Leanna and I managed to get away by ourselves and noon at Alcove Spring. We spread a blanket on a flat rock and watched the falling waters sparkle in the sunlight, sharing dried apples and bread that Aunt Tamsen had baked that morning. Leanna knew I was uneasy about Grandma, so she kept me laughing with one funny story after another about her family.

"You're lucky to have so many sisters and cousins," I remarked, blinking at the reflection of light on the pool.

Leanna wound her long braid around her fingers. Her brow furrowed and her smile disappeared. "It's because there are so many Donner parents," she said.

I raised my eyebrows.

"Aunt Betsy was married before she married Uncle Jake. Their two oldest aren't really his. Just the younger five."

"Oh. Just the younger *five.*" I laughed.

But Leanna's expression didn't change. "My ma, the one you call Aunt Tamsen, isn't my real mother." Her voice softened. "I had a real mother, but she died when I was little."

I shifted my weight on the hard rock. "That's sad."

"She's *almost* my real mother, and the little girls are my half sisters, but"—she looked away—"sometimes I don't think she loves me same as them."

I hadn't noticed Aunt Tamsen treating Leanna any different from her sisters. Surely Leanna was wrong. I wanted to tell her so, but my thoughts turned to the daguerreotype that Mama kept in our family Bible. The newfangled photographic image was taken a year after Tommy was born. It showed my family grouped in the Springfield parlor, staring solemnly into the camera. Everyone—even my parents—looked alike, with their dark hair and sharp chins. And then there was me, Virginia. Round face, light-brown hair, gray eyes.

"It's the same with me," I said.

Leanna turned to me questioningly.

"My real father died of cholera after I was born. But Pa says I'm his daughter now. He married Mama when I was still a baby. We came as a package, he says."

Leanna started winding her braid again. "Then I guess you feel like I do—like he doesn't love you same as Patty and your brother."

I didn't answer right away. I was lost in my first memory of Pa and me—riding with him in front of the house the day he bought Glaucus. After that, I rode with him every day. We rode to his furniture factory on the Sangamon River, where Milt stopped his work to greet me; to the city bank, where Pa sat me on the counter while he talked with the bankers; and to the shops, where merchants fussed over me and gave me candy.

On my eighth birthday, Pa lifted me off Glaucus for the last time. "You're too big to ride with me anymore," he said.

Before I could protest, he put his finger to his lips, took my hand, and walked me into the barn. Mama stood in the shadows, holding three-year-old Patty's hand and stroking a pony with liquid-brown eyes.

"Meet Billy," Pa said.

"Puss?" Leanna poked me with her elbow. "Have you ever felt like he doesn't love—"

"No," I said, remembering the joy on Pa's face at that moment. "Never. Never ever."

I rose and shook my skirt free of crumbs. I didn't want Leanna to see the tears that had sprung to my eyes.

Could Pa really stop loving me if I became a Catholic? Would he disown me? He'd as much as said so. The idea was so frightening that my rosary necklace was back in its shell case.

I would stay a Methodist like Pa and the rest of my family.

On our third afternoon at Alcove Spring, camp buzzed with the news that the raft was nearly complete. I walked Tommy to a clearing near the river to take a look.

Milt and the other builders had set logs side by side and fastened them together by nailing long boards across each end. Then they hollowed out two more logs into canoe-like pontoons and attached them to the raft to help it float. Milt, standing beside us with thumbs through his suspenders, grinned proudly as the men attached a long rope to the raft and staked it to our side of the river. Several others swam their horses across the river and staked the other end of the rope to the opposite bank.

Milt gave me his crooked smile. "No need to be scared this time, Puss. We're going to *pull* it back and forth. It can't be swept downriver."

I trusted Milt, who took such pride in his work when he was foreman at Pa's furniture factory. As the men pushed the tethered raft into the river, Milt rocked back and forth on his big feet, beaming at Tommy. "We've christened it the 'River Rover,'" he said. "We'll be ready to cross tomorrow morning."

But that night Grandma had a coughing spell that went on past midnight. Pa sat her up and gave her a shot of whiskey. Mama rubbed her back and gave her sugar cubes. I gave her a cup of cold water. Grandma coughed everything back up.

Mama finally told us children to get into bed. Patty and Tommy slept beside me soundly through the night, but I stared into the darkness of the canvas ceiling, waiting through each stretch of silence for the next round of coughing, and wincing each time it came. I thought about Mama's near silence all day while tending to Grandma, and my suspicion grew into the realization that Grandma had something far worse than a bad cold.

I yearned to hold my rosary while I prayed for her. But instead I whispered every prayer I'd ever learned at Methodist Sunday school, then whispered them all again.

Grandma slept through my morning routine of preparing breakfast. When she finally woke, her smile was weak and her eyes were dull. She wouldn't eat.

I patted the crusty patches along her lids and mouth with a damp cloth. Then I slid her specs over her nose and behind her ears.

"I'll stay like this for awhile longer, dear," she said when I tried to help her sit up. "You run along."

Mama hadn't slept a wink all night. Now she sat on the patchwork quilt near the river, absently petting little Cash who napped alongside her. Her looped braids, usually neatly woven, were losing wisps of hair to the mild breeze.

"Here, Mama. Be careful, this is hot." I handed her a cup of black coffee, then sat beside her, yawning.

Mama cradled her cup as she watched the livestock drink their fill of the river. She took a long breath and turned to me. Her eyes were bloodshot, her nose red. "I want to prepare you, Puss. Your grandma isn't going to make it further."

Suddenly I was fully alert. "What? I just talked to her, Mama. I think she's getting better."

Mama shook her head. "It's consumption," she said.

This couldn't be. Consumption. One of the deadly diseases of Springfield that we were supposed to be leaving behind.

"You know your grandmother insisted on coming, even though we all well knew she might not make it to California," Mama continued.

I nodded, my heart sinking. I *did* know. It was one of the many reasons Uncle Jim hadn't wanted us to go.

I tugged at a clump of wet grass and threw it back onto the ground. Why was Mama telling me this?

As if reading my mind, she said, "You're my eldest, Puss. I'm going to need you to be strong. Especially for Patty."

Patty. Patty and Grandma. Patty's heart would break if Grandma died. I bit down on my lower lip to keep the tears back.

Mama and I sat together in silence, listening to morning sounds: the low hum of men's conversations, the clink of metal dishes being washed, Aunt Betsy calling out for her children. In time Mama stood with a sigh, smoothed her skirt, and started toward the family wagon, Cash following her.

I folded the quilt and hugged it to my body. Life without Grandma was too sad to contemplate. But a flicker of importance lay beneath the sadness. Mama had just seen fit to confide in me, even ask for my help, as though I were another grownup.

Pa talked Colonel Russell into staying at Alcove Spring a bit longer, and word about Grandma's condition spread through the company. A handful of mean-spirited men, Pa told me, were angered by the delay. But sympathetic women came by with elixirs and family cures. Mrs. Breen presented Mama with a syrupy concoction she swore by. "It's an old Irish recipe. If it doesn't work, then 'tis God's will, 'tis," she said earnestly.

Grandma died that night while we children slept.

The next morning Grandma's blue-flowered quilt covered her from head to toe. I stayed inside with Patty and Tommy while kind families stopped by to tell my parents how sorry they were. Mama, standing outside the family wagon beside Pa, thanked the women while Pa carried on long, low-voiced conversations with the men. I felt stunned with grief but, remembering Mama's request, did my best to comfort Patty and answer Tommy's questions.

"Are we going to take her home now?" Tommy asked me, sneaking a curious peek at Grandma's bed. He knew where Grandpa Keyes and our baby brother Gerson were buried. Mama had made us visit their graves in the Methodist cemetery one last time before we left Springfield.

"No, Tommy. We have to bury her here."

"We can't bury Grandma out *here*." Patty lifted her tearstained face. "Injuns'll dig her up."

Tommy began to wail, and I silently cursed Aunt Betsy's son Will. A few days earlier he'd told Patty and me that Indians dug up pioneer graves. They did it to steal things, he said. Jackets, shoes, even hair ribbons.

Just then Colonel Russell's voice boomed outside the wagon. "Don't you worry, Mrs. Reed." I pictured the portly, white-bearded man peering down at Mama and clasping her hands in his large ones. "We won't be crossing the river today. We've suspended all activities. We'll hold a beautiful service for your mother this afternoon."

Nearly every member of the Russell Party attended Grandma's service. Papa read the twenty-third Psalm from our family Bible. Hundreds of voices rose through the trees with "Nearer My God to Thee." Through it all, Milt stood with the family—Mr. Stanton, too. That night I was stirred to pick up a quill pen and write.

> My Dear Couzin … We came to the blue the Water was so hye we had to stay thare 4 days in the mean time gramma died…We buried her verry decent We made a nete coffin and buried her under a tree we had a head stone and had her name cutonit, and the date and yere verry nice, and at the head of the grave was a tree we cut some letters on it the young men soded it all ofer and put Flores on it We miss her verry much evry time we come in the wagon we look up at the bed for her…

SEVEN

JUNE 1846. MOVING ON.

I walked with Patty alongside the family wagon. Pa and Mama walked ahead with Tommy and little Cash. The afternoon air was unseasonably chilly, the sky overcast. Ten days earlier we'd crossed the Big Blue—without Grandma. Being together all day was a comfort now. Pa and I didn't ride off for hours anymore. Mama ignored her needlework and let the mending pile up. Both wore long faces and hovered over us children.

We were near the middle of the caravan today. Wagons flowed ahead and behind as far as I could see, and wheels squeaked and rattled as they turned on the rutted trail. We moved over a bleak, treeless plateau separating the Big Blue from the next river we would follow, the Platte. Fine dirt powdered my boots with each step, coating the toes and laces. The sun peeked briefly through gray clouds, warming my face, then hiding again. As long as I kept walking, I didn't need my coat.

Patty clutched my hand. I glanced at her now and then, but her face was downcast. She hadn't talked much since Grandma's death, and I didn't want to coax her. I was thinking my own sad thoughts—wondering how long it would take Uncle Jim and Aunt Lydia to get the letter Pa had entrusted to an eastbound traveler, and how they would break the bad news about

Grandma to Mary. My own letter to Mary was in my pocket, far too short to send just yet.

Not only my family was disheartened. Other families were fretting about our slow progress. Before we left Springfield, Pa told us we should cross the Sierra Nevada Mountains into California by late September to avoid the chance of early snows. But the spring rains and high rivers had put us two weeks behind schedule.

When folks weren't blaming the weather for our slowness, they were blaming Colonel Russell's leadership, pointing out that several other wagon trains had passed us by. And, Mrs. Breen told Mama, some were actually blaming Pa, claiming the heaviness of our family wagon was slowing the entire company down. Pa laughed it off, telling us children that most other families envied all we had.

We did have more than other families. Some had no horses at all, and of those who did, none had one as fine as Glaucus. Eyebrows shot up whenever Pa rode her through camp. Most families had only one wagon, while we, the Donner families, and the Breens each had three. Our family wagon, with its spring sofas and wood-burning stove, drew sarcastic comments instead of compliments. A few of the women had nicknamed it the "pioneer palace car" back at Alcove Spring. They hadn't meant the name to be a compliment, but when word got around to Pa, he thought it quite fitting, so soon we were calling our family wagon the palace car, too.

Maybe our family wagon *was* a bit too big, I thought as I squeezed Patty's hand, but at least the River Rover had floated it over the Big Blue without incident. We'd crossed the day after Grandma's service. By then the river had receded several feet, so the hardest part of the crossing was the sure knowledge we were leaving Grandma behind forever.

"Ah-choo!" The powdery dirt stirred up by oxen hooves and turning wheels found its way into my nose, jolting me from my musings. I sneezed again as Uncle George and Mr. Stanton, who'd been scouting ahead, rode up to my parents.

Mr. Stanton exclaimed over an antelope herd he'd spotted. I could hear him only in bits. Uncle George's gravelly voice was louder. "Only a mile or so 'til we reach the Great Plains," he said. Then he rode past Patty and me, winking as he continued down the wagon train to spread the news. Mr. Stanton stayed, dismounting Banjo to walk alongside my parents. Their three heads bent and nodded in grownup conversation. I strained to hear, then gave up and watched instead.

Mama looked thinner, but maybe that was because she'd shed most of her petticoats and had taken to hitching up her skirts to keep the hems from getting dirty. Pa and Mr. Stanton both wore narrow-brimmed hats, long-sleeve cotton shirts, and wide suspenders that held up their britches, but Mr. Stanton was shorter than Pa by a head. He was describing something to my parents, nodding and waving his arms.

Everyone in the Russell Company liked Mr. Stanton. While my family kept to a small circle of acquaintances, Mr. Stanton talked to anyone who would listen. He didn't take part in petty quarrels and finger pointing—he was too engaged in explaining river flows or animal life. When he wasn't riding with Pa and me, he was collecting rocks and plants. And, like Aunt Tamsen, he drew pictures of the wildflowers we passed by.

I pricked up my ears. People were yelling up ahead. Whooping. Hollering, too. Mr. Stanton turned and smiled.

"What's happening?" I called out.

"Sounds like we've reached Nebraska territory, girls. The Great Plains."

Those who'd been walking ahead were now running toward the plateau's edge.

"Ho-ly *Moses!*" I heard a boy yell. Then a chorus of voices— even deep men's voices—oohed and aahed.

Patty and I looked at each other and, still holding hands, took off running. We were out of breath by the time we reached the front of the wagon train and worked our way through the crowd. Our eyes followed the plateau's long, downward slope.

Patty squeezed my hand. "Oh, my, Puss," she said. "It's—it looks like heaven, don't you think?"

Rolling out before us was a flat, emerald-green valley that extended and blurred into the horizon. The expanse was split by the widest river yet—even wider than the Missouri. Slow-moving waters wove around its wooded islands like intricate braids. Sunlight sparkled on its surface.

Pa and Mr. Stanton walked up behind us. "Well, I'll be," Pa said. "A mile wide and an inch deep. That's what they say about the Platte River."

I pointed to a faraway dust cloud that appeared to be moving across the valley floor. I turned to Mr. Stanton. "What is that?"

He shaded his brow. "That, young lady, is a buffalo herd. The plains are teeming with them. Antelope, too."

I squinted, trying to see what he could see. Leave it to Mr. Stanton, who'd never been west of Illinois, to identify a buffalo herd from this far.

"Here, Mr. Reed." Milt handed Pa the brass field glass from our wagon. "You can get a closer look with this."

Pa pulled the glass out to its full length and held it to his eye. "Oh, my—look at them all!"

"How about it, Mr. Reed?" Milt asked, hands in his pockets. "Are you going to try your luck with the rifle?"

Pa chuckled and handed the glass to Mr. Stanton. "I just may, Milt. We could use something other than dried beef and beans for our supper."

Mr. Stanton peered through the field glass, gave a long, low whistle, then handed it to me. I turned the glass until I got a clear view of the stately animals. They were crossing the river, bending their heavy heads to drink as they moved.

"There are hundreds of them!" I said. "Babies, too."

"Babies!" Patty squeaked. "Let me see!" She grabbed for the glass. I lifted it over my head, hoping to look a few minutes more.

"Please, Puss!" The light was back in Patty's eyes. Relenting, I bent down and held the glass as she looked through the eyepiece.

"Ooh." Patty grinned up at me. "Baby buffalo." She looked through the glass again. "Puss, did you see all those flowers down there?"

"Thousands," I said, relieved to see her smiling again.

Mama and Tommy walked up behind us, and the oohing and aahing started all over again.

I felt like a great weight was lifting from my family. Surely the worst of this journey was behind us. Our future was like this valley—full of promise and possibility.

I held the glass for Tommy next. "Is that California?" he asked.

Pa threw his head back and laughed. "We have a ways to go yet, son. These plains stretch four hundred miles, all the way to the Rockies. But we're in for a long, easy ride 'til then. This is where we'll make up for lost time."

EIGHT

JUNE 1846. THE GREAT PLAINS.

"Our journey so far has been pleasant, the roads have been good, and food plentiful...Wood is now very scarce, but 'buffalo chips' are excellent; they kindle quickly and retain heat surprisingly."

Aunt Tamsen looked up from reading her letter aloud and smiled. "I wonder what the editors of the *Sangamon Journal* will think of that," she said. "Who'd have thought we'd be using buffalo dung for fuel!"

We were into our second week on the Great Plains. The mercury in Pa's thermometer was at eighty-three degrees, and a group of us had finished picnicking side by side on quilts in a narrow strip of shade by the palace car. The sky was a brilliant blue; puffy white clouds floated high above. A man traveling east had camped with us the night before, and now several grownups were writing letters for him to carry to a general store in Independence. From there, Mama explained, travelers would volunteer to deliver the letters to Springfield as they moved farther east.

Leanna and I were leaning against a nearby wagon. Leanna bent down and peered at her mother's letter. "What else did you say?"

Aunt Tamsen continued reading in her schoolteacher tone:

> "The Indians frequently come to see us, and the chiefs of a tribe breakfasted at our tent this morning. All are so friendly that I cannot help feeling sympathy and friendship for them."

She lowered the page to her lap. "That should raise some eyebrows back home."

Small groups of curious Pawnee men had taken to riding into camp every day. Their chests were bare and their heads were shaved, except for one long lock of hair. They wore simple loincloths with leather leggings.

Most everyone in the company traded with them—buttons for reed baskets, whiskey for animal skins. When one old Pawnee man noticed children staring at his beaded moccasins, he rode off for a few hours and then returned with several tiny imitations to trade for coffee. Mama got a pair for Tommy, then traded a box of sugar cubes for a longhaired buffalo robe.

"We'll be glad to have this when the weather gets colder," she said as I helped her stuff the heavy hide into the supply wagon. She wrinkled her nose. "Even though it smells some."

Pa was writing a letter, too. I left Leanna's side to sit next to him. "Are you writing to Uncle Jim?"

Pa nodded and continued to scribble.

"Read some of it," I urged, sidling up to him. "Please."

Pa held out the sheet of paper, a gleam in his eye.

"I have to compete with old experienced hunters, and re-move the stars from their brows. Knowing that Glaucus could beat any horse on the Nebraska, I came to the conclusion that as far as buffalo killing was concerned, I could beat them."

"Your boastful spirit is showing again, James." Mama shook her head in disapproval, but kept her eyes on her own letter. "My brother won't believe a word."

Pa grinned and continued reading aloud.

"This is my greatest ambition, to show them I have the best horse in the company, and that I am the best and most daring horseman in the caravan."

"Oh, that *is* too prideful, Pa!" I laughed. But what he'd written was true. No other horse in the company *could* outrun Glaucus, and Pa was providing us, as well as the Donner and Breen fami-lies, with buffalo steaks every night. Still, I was beginning to un-derstand why Pa's need to be the best at everything—a long-held joke within the family—might seem like arrogance to company members who didn't know him as well as we did.

Mr. Stanton, sitting cross-legged next to Pa, seemed un-aware of the conversation around him. He was writing his own letter.

"What about you, Charlie?" I asked uncertainly. Since Mr. Stanton was now a family friend, Mama had given me permission to call him by his first name. It still sounded a bit forward to me.

"Puss," Mama said. "Perhaps Charlie doesn't want to say..."

Charlie raised his head and adjusted his glasses. "It's all right. I'm writing to my brother and sister-in-law in New York."

He smiled directly at me. "They think I'm still in Chicago." He glanced over the page for moment, and then began to read aloud.

> "I met with a good opportunity and, thinking it doubtful whether I should find anything to do in this country I concluded to go.... if you have never read Hastings' Oregon & California, get it and read it. You will see some of the inducements which led me to this step."

Lansford Hastings. That was the name of the author of that yellow-covered book Pa quoted from so often over the past year, the book that encouraged him to give up everything and move us all to California.

I scanned the scores of wagons scattered across the prairie like so many dandelions. "I guess a lot of men read Mr. Hastings' book," I murmured.

Mama looked up from her letter to Aunt Lydia. "Aren't you going to write a letter to Mary, dear? You may not get another chance to get one delivered until we reach Fort Laramie."

The letter I'd begun to Mary at Alcove Spring was still in my pocket. I knew she could read my spelling, but what if she took my letter to school? Would Mrs. Roark tsk-tsk and shake her head in that disappointed way of hers? Would my old schoolmates laugh at my mangled words? My face went hot just thinking about it.

"I need more time," I said, standing up and brushing imaginary crumbs from my skirt. "Let's walk to the river, Leanna."

Though we traveled up to fifteen miles a day through unchanging surroundings, the plains were alive with movement. The sky arched over us like a blue dome, and clouds cast shadows over the flatlands and plateaus as they sailed by. Wildflowers of every color mingled and swayed with the tall grasses, and the air was sweet with their fragrance. The temperature rose to ninety degrees, but a breeze off the river kept me cool as I rode Billy beside it.

We chased the strange barking squirrels that darted in and out of the ground. Pa called them prairie dogs.

"Stay away from those dog holes," he'd warn as they burrowed into the earth. "Billy could break a leg in one of those."

Sometimes there was a slithery movement through the grass ahead. "Keep a lookout for snakes," he'd say. "Those rattlers are poisonous."

But the beauty of the plains overshadowed the dangers.

"How are we going to cross this one, Pa?" We'd stopped the horses on the riverbank to watch a snowy egret snatch fish from the slow current.

Pa adjusted his hat to shade his brow. He studied the mile-wide waters. "The worst of the rivers are behind us, Puss," he said. "The Platte may be wide, but when the time comes, we can probably cross it on foot."

I gazed at the grass meeting the sky in every direction; geese flying against the sun, their silhouettes spiraling over wooded islands; and here and there in the distance, a hazy bluff. Patty is right, I thought. It *does* look like heaven.

Uncle George or Ed Breen sometimes rode with Pa and me. Charlie joined us, too. Since Banjo, with his stocky build and short legs, wasn't as fast as our horses, Pa and I would slow Billy and Glaucus down to a walk, and the two men would share their plans for California. That's how I learned Pa was going to help our teamster Milt claim his very own land in California. Charlie talked about opening a general store like the one he'd had in Chicago, "Only successful this time," he said, giving me a wink.

"Business in California will be booming!" Pa assured him.

Wouldn't Charlie's store have to be in a city? How often would I see him if our new home was in the country? I started to ask if he planned to settle near us, but a confusing wave of shyness overtook me, and I said nothing.

By our third week on the plains, I wanted to stay.

"Why go all the way to California?" I asked Pa one afternoon. We were following the trail through a shallow, wet section of meadow. A flock of sandhill cranes rose in front of us, their huge wings beating in slow rythym.

Pa didn't answer. He'd been grouchy ever since a run-in that morning with a German emigrant named Mr. Keseberg.

Pa had finally given in to Colonel Russell's requests to lighten the palace car. He and Milt were lifting a small, but heavy, box of Grandma's belongings out the side door as I stood nearby, my bag of washed dishes beside me.

"Is dat all you're leaving behind, Reed?" I turned when I recognized the German accent. Mr. Keseberg, a blond, big-shouldered man with light blue eyes, sat astride his horse. His full lips sneered beneath his mustache. "Seems to me you can afford to unload a fair amount more. Da rest of us would surely appreciate it." My throat tightened as I looked back at Pa.

"You tend to your business, Keseberg," Pa answered in that level, controlled tone of his. He didn't look up. "And I'll tend to mine."

Although the Russell Company was a moving city of nearly a hundred families, I didn't know many beside those who rotated through the line with us. I likened it to a neighborhood—the Donner families, the Breens, and the Kesebergs. But Pa didn't like Mr. Keseberg; he said he was mean-spirited. We children avoided him whenever we could.

The Kesebergs traveled with a kindly, leather-faced old man everyone called Hardcoop. Hardcoop had a toothless smile and a few wispy tufts of white hair growing from his freckled head. He knew most of the little ones by name and spent much of his time whittling toys while telling them funny stories about his boyhood in Belgium.

"Patty dear," he called out when Patty and I walked past the Keseberg wagon that very same evening, "You and your big sister come over here. I got somethin' for ya."

Patty took off running. I followed more slowly, reminding myself I would soon be thirteen—almost a grownup. Hardcoop held out a small, rough-hewn wooden horse. "Think that little brother of yours would like this?"

"Thank you, Mr. Hardcoop," Patty said. She held it up. "Look, Puss. Now Tommy has a pony, like you." But her face was full of disappointment.

"Now, Patty dear, I didn't forget you." Hardcoop winked at me as he reached into his shirt pocket. He pulled out a tiny carved doll with painted black hair and eyes, and a red bow mouth. "I thought you might like a little friend to play with. Isn't she pretty?"

Patty's face lit up. "She's beautiful."

The old man flashed a pink-gum smile. "I couldn't carve her no pretty dresses, but I'm sure your big sister here can sew her some."

Just then Mr. Keseberg poked his head out of the wagon. "You loudmouth Reed girls should learn to keep your voices down," he snapped. "Get on home, now. My young one is sleeping."

His words fell like a sharp slap. Patty flinched. My heart hammered as I hurried her back to the palace car.

"Please, Patty, don't tell Pa about this." My voice shook. "We don't want trouble with Mr. Keseberg."

Then I remembered another line from Aunt Tamsen's letter:

> "We have the best of people in our company, and some, too, that are not so good."

NINE

JUNE 1846. THE WARNING.

F ort Laramie was a fur-trading outpost protected by high
adobe walls and a watchtower. Tepees dotted the land surrounding it. I counted eighty of the cone-shaped tents as we
rode toward the fort, then gave up, realizing that there were
at least twice that many more. Besides, my attention was sidetracked by Sioux women cooking over their campfires.

They looked nothing like the poor Caw women who stood
outside a store back in Independence. The Sioux were tall and
stately, with bright feathers and ribbons wound through black
hair. Their simple fringed dresses were made of soft buckskin,
and their feet were covered with intricately beaded moccasins.

"I don't see any *man* Indians, Pa. Where are they?"

Pa dismounted Glaucus and studied our surroundings.
"They can't all be inside the fort," he said. "They're hunting,
most likely."

The company set up wagon circles opposite the teepees.
Near sunset, several of us gathered outside our circle as a
stream of Sioux men rode in from the hunt, their horses
weighed down with slaughtered buffalo parts. They too wore
clothing of buckskin adorned with beads.

"The Sioux are the prettiest-dressed Indians I've ever seen," I declared.

"And grand figures on horseback," Pa added. "But I wonder why so many are gathered here. This place is more like a Sioux village than a trading post."

Mr. Breen overheard Pa's remark. "I was inside the fort earlier," he said. "It's like a small town in there. Word is they are preparin' for war with the Crow tribe."

I looked up at Mr. Breen's freckly face. "They brought their families to a war?"

"Maybe it's too dangerous to leave them behind, unprotected," Pa said. He picked up Tommy and held him close. "I just hope they fight their battles far from us."

That evening a number of Sioux families visited our wagon circle. Several campfires and dozens of lanterns lit the scene while they traded with company members. I encouraged Tommy to approach a little Indian boy, and soon they were playing tag like children everywhere.

Leanna and I watched the boys' game from the back of one of the Donner wagons. Our parents sat nearby, sharing a fire with the Breens and several other families.

"Puss, that boy over there is staring," Leanna said. I turned. A Sioux boy with broad flat features and high cheekbones was standing near Billy, watching us. A single feather rose from the back of his head. His dark braids dropped past his shoulders onto a buckskin shirt. His deep-set eyes locked on mine for an instant. Unsure, I gave him a hesitant wave. He looked away and started petting Billy's cream-colored neck.

I felt my face flush. "Maybe he's shy," I said.

Leanna giggled. "He looks like an exotic prince from one of my mother's books."

I turned to look again, but the Indian boy was gone.

"Reed!" An unkempt man in dirty buckskins strode out of the dark toward the campfire. "My word. James Reed! Some folks who passed you up last week told me you was on this trail. I hoped to meet you here."

Pa rose. "Why, it's Jim Clyman," he exclaimed. The two men shook hands. "What are you doing here? Sit down. Meet my family."

I grabbed Leanna's hand as we jumped from the wagon and hurried over. Pa explained that he and Mr. Clyman had served together in the Black Hawk War of 1832, a series of battles between Indians and the US Army over land in Illinois. As Pa poured the mountain man a glass of whiskey, I wondered how the two of them could ever have been friends. Mr. Clyman was nothing like Pa's business friends in Springfield. He was more like the trappers in Independence—disheveled men who looked as though they never washed. So I was surprised when Mama, who would normally keep her distance from someone so rough, greeted him warmly. "My husband has told me stories about your time together," she said. "Have you been living out West all these years since?"

Mr. Clyman explained he'd been working as a trapper in the Rocky Mountains. "But I've spent the past year in California."

"Why did you leave?" Pa asked. "You can claim land there now."

Mr. Clyman shook his head. "Don't like it there. Too many pioneers movin' in and spoiling everything. I'm going home to Wisconsin."

Pa seemed dumbstruck for a moment. Then he asked, "Have you heard of a man named Lansford Hastings?"

Other conversations around the campfire came to a halt. The men leaned in closer.

"Heard of 'im," Mr. Clyman answered. "I *know* 'im."

"You do? You know him?" Pa's eyes lit up. He leaned forward. "Well, some of us here have read his book. We're considering the cutoff he describes. The one that starts at Fort Bridger and goes south of the Salt Lake."

Mr. Clyman snorted. "The Hastings Cutoff, he calls it. Named it after hisself. I scouted it from California to Fort Bridger a couple months ago." He took a swig of whiskey, then looked around. "Hastings promoted that cutoff without traveling it first, you know that? It's thick with brush. I barely got through, and I was on horseback."

"But his book was published last year," Pa said. "He wouldn't have suggested a route he hadn't tried himself."

Mr. Clyman ignored this. "It's nearing July, Reed," he said. "You've come only six hundred fifty miles since you left Independence. You're running late, and you gotta cross the Sierra before winter. Stay on the main trail like everyone else."

Pa shifted uncomfortably, and I became aware that others at the campfire were hanging on to every word between the two men.

"There's no need for us to take such a roundabout route," Pa said. "Not when there's a shorter one."

Mr. Clyman finished off his whiskey. "Listen, boys," he said. "I know you want to save as many miles as you can. But you'll have a hell of a time getting these wagons through the Wasatch Mountains. And if you do, then God help you, because then you'll be on the Great Salt Desert, the most desolate country on the continent."

"But Hastings wrote—"

"Dang it, Reed! I know what Hastings wrote, and I'm telling you, it ain't true. Anything can happen out there. Anything."

Mr. Clyman's words sent a tremor through me. But Pa set his mouth in a stubborn line. He didn't believe his old friend, and I thought I knew why. Lansford Hastings' book had served us well so far. Hadn't he thoroughly explained how to outfit a wagon and what items to bring? Hadn't he correctly described the beauty of the plains, the friendliness of the Indians, and the endless supply of buffalo meat? Pa tried to change the subject, but Mr. Clyman must have sensed his warning was ignored. As he stood to say his good-byes, he seemed more sad than angry.

The Sioux eventually left camp for their teepees. Most company members went to bed, but those of us around the Donner campfire stayed awhile longer.

Mr. Breen took Mr. Clyman's words to heart. "That settles 'er. I'm not taking my family over that so-called shortcut," he said, getting up to leave. "Too dangerous."

He and Mrs. Breen walked off, and a heated discussion between Pa and the Donner brothers followed. From time to time I exchanged questioning looks with Leanna. Why couldn't the grownups agree on something so important?

"Clyman's mistaken," Pa declared, finally standing to leave. "The cutoff is still our best bet."

I said goodnight to Leanna and followed my parents back to the palace car.

"James, why are you so sure he's wrong?" I heard Mama ask as they passed the Breen family wagon. "You always spoke well of Mr. Clyman."

"I've read all there is to read about the cutoff, Margaret." Pa's tone held an irritated edge. "I've studied all the maps. I wouldn't put you or the children in danger."

"I know that, James, but—"

I slowed my step, falling farther behind. Now even my parents were arguing about the best way to get to California.

"I believe in the Holy Spirit, the Holy Catholic Church, the communion of Saints, the forgiveness of sins, the resurrection of the body, and life everlasting."

The voice was Mr. Breen's. His words stirred something inside me, and I stopped next to his wagon. Mrs. Breen's strident voice chimed in, along with the children's.

"As it was in the beginning, is now, and ever shall be, world without end."

Was this part of the Rosary? I stood very still and listened, yearning for the comfort of my hidden-away necklace.

The next morning I woke to the smell of coffee. The sun shone through the canvas ceiling, and I was already too warm. Tommy slept next to me, a jumble of little arms and legs, beads of sweat on his forehead.

Outside, men called out as they watered the livestock, dogs barked for scraps of food, and women spoke softly as they cooked over camp stoves.

Most days started out like this. But today was different. It was June 28th: my thirteenth birthday.

I climbed out of bed and pulled on my sun-faded blue plaid dress, then glanced across the wagon. Mama and Patty were already outside. Good. Now I could study my image for a few minutes without appearing vain. I peered into the mirror, half expecting to see someone a bit different from the twelve-year-old who left Springfield three months earlier.

Did my face look older? I was thinner—my cheekbones were more noticeable. I removed my hairpins and unbraided my hair. It fell halfway down my back, and despite the protection of my bonnet, had a reddish hue from full days in the sun.

I'd grown taller, too. "Good gracious, Puss," Mama had said recently as we walked together beside the wagon. "You're looking nearly straight into my eyes."

But most noticeable were the changes taking place beneath my dress. My chest was beginning to push against my bodice. My arms and legs were filling out, too.

Was I becoming pretty? I peered in closer. I didn't look much like Mama or Patty, with their porcelain skin and dark hair, and I didn't have beautiful eyes like Leanna. But boys in the company had begun to notice me. A longhaired, skinny boy about my age had asked me to dance at campfire a few nights ago. I blushed and shook my head, while Leanna clapped a hand over her mouth and giggled. And just last week Pa had spoken sharply to an older boy who tried to ride beside me.

I was distracted from the mirror by the scent of sizzling johnnycakes. Was I imagining things? For days now, breakfast had been only bacon and coffee. I quickly rebraided my hair and stepped down the stairs. Pa, Mama, and Patty were huddled around the camp stove, hypnotized by small, bubbling rounds of batter. Pa smiled up at me, and Mama said, "Hello, birthday girl. We couldn't bake you a cake this year, so johnnycakes will have to do."

I smiled back, relieved. The tension between my parents must have melted away during the night.

"How did you do this?" I huddled between them, my mouth watering. "I thought we ran out of cornmeal weeks ago."

Mama's smile broadened. She nodded toward the fort. "Your father went shopping. He bought honey, too."

Pa reached over and hugged me with one arm. He was as pleased about the johnnycakes as I was. "Happy birthday, Puss. Now get your brother out here so we can eat."

I had barely savored my first bite of the warm, sweet cakes when Patty handed me a package loosely wrapped in a striped dishcloth and tied with blue yarn. "I made part of this."

Inside was a yellow sunbonnet. The brim was trimmed in brown lace, and a long piece of fabric was attached to the back.

"Grandma started it," Patty said. "She stitched every day when you were out riding with Pa. She made the flap extra long to cover the back of your neck." Her face darkened as she added, "But then Mama had to finish it."

"Notice the laced edging?" Mama said, pulling Patty close. "Patty did that. When you were out riding, Grandma taught her to crochet."

"Really? You made this lace, Patty? It's beautiful!"

Patty looked down at her hands, a smile tugging at the corner of her mouth.

I pictured Grandma sitting in her feather bed, watching the prairie go by and stitching a bonnet for my birthday. I saw Patty sitting beside her, practicing the complicated movements of a tiny hook over fine thread. I imagined Mama and Patty hurrying to finish the bonnet together whenever I was off with Pa. My heart swelled up.

"It's very dear. I'll wear it every day from now on," I said, and hugged them both.

"This is from Pa and me," Tommy said, handing me a pair of supple leather boots, gathered at the ankle and laced with cord.

"Sioux moccasins!" I examined the bright patterns. "Hundreds of beads, and even tiny shells." I looked up, beaming. "I'm saving these for California."

"I bought them just this morning," Pa said. "From an Indian who made an offer on Billy."

"An offer?" My smile faded. "What do you mean?"

Pa explained that a Sioux man had approached him at daybreak and offered the moccasins for the cream-colored pony his son had seen at campfire.

"I saw that boy. He was petting Billy!" I flushed with indignation. "No, Pa!"

"No, Pa!" Patty and Tommy yelled in unison.

"Don't worry. I *bought* these from him instead"—he gestured toward the moccasins—"and sent him on his way. Billy's still yours."

"That boy had better not try to steal my pony," I said under my breath.

Just then Charlie strode up, carrying a bunch of wildflowers.

"I heard the commotion over here, and wanted to wish you a happy birthday," he said, thrusting the bouquet at me.

No one, not even Pa, had ever given me flowers. I felt the color rise to my cheeks.

"These are so nice," I blurted out, half expecting Charlie to explain why iris and honeysuckle grow wild on the plains. But he merely nodded, his kind eyes smiling through his glasses.

TEN

JULY 1846. INDEPENDENCE ROCK.

"James, what is that paper you keep reading?" Mama peered at Pa over her coffee as we children finished up our cornmeal mush.

We had crossed the Platte River and were now camped on sage-covered sand near Independence Rock, a granite outcrop that was a half-mile long and more than a hundred feet high. Patty and I agreed the rock looked like a giant, lopsided turtle. A hundred miles to the west, the Rocky Mountains hovered like a wavy shadow.

Pa leaned back from the campfire and grinned as though he'd won a hand at poker. He folded the paper and slid it into his shirt pocket.

"It's our passport to California, Margaret," he said. "A letter from Lansford Hastings. That rider going east, Mr. Bonney, delivered this to Colonel Russell last night."

My ears perked up. I knew the rider was moving on later today. He'd agreed to carry letters home for us, including the letter to Mary I started at Alcove Spring when Grandma died. I added to it when we were on the plains and finished it first thing this morning. I pulled the letter from my skirt pocket and reread hastily, searching for misspellings.

"the sowe Indians are the pretest drest Indians thare is Paw goes a bufalo hunting most every day and kils 2 or 3 buffalo every day paw shot a elk som of our compan saw a grisly bear We have the thermometer 102° - average for the last 6 days"

I sighed and shook my head. Imaginary letters were so much easier to write. Imaginary letters were perfect, with no misspellings or crossed-out words.

Mama's voice broke through my thoughts. "Don't worry about your spelling, dear. Your father can look your letter over before he gives it to Mr. Bonney."

How long had she been watching? And how did she know I was checking my spelling?

"My spelling's fine, Mama. I don't want anyone but Mary to read it, anyway."

"We selabrated the 4 of July on plat at bever criek several of the Gentemen in Springfield gave paw a botel of licker and said it shoulden be opend tell the 4 day of July and paw was to look to the east and drink it and thay was to look to the West an drink it at 12 oclock paw treted the company and we all had some leminade. maw and pau is well and sends there best love to you all. I send my best love to you all—"

I squinted critically at the words. Some were surely wrong, because I'd spelled them two or three different ways in the same letter. I had no idea which way was right.

"—I am a going to send this letter by a man coming from oregon by his self he is going to take his family back to

oregon We are all doing Well and in hye sperits so I must
close yur letter. You are fo ever my affectionate couzen."

I sighed again, dissatisfied. But at least I'd kept my promise to Mary; I'd written her a letter from the trail. I added
"Independence rock July th12 1846," at the top, refolded it, and
handed it to Pa.

"I don't want anyone but Mary to read it," I repeated.

Pa nodded distractedly, his eyes on Mama. "Hastings writes
that he's at Fort Bridger, waiting to lead a wagon train over that
cutoff."

Mama set down her cup and looked him in the eye. "You
know how I feel about that shortcut, James."

"You've no reason to fear it now," Pa assured her. "Not with
Hastings leading us." He gestured toward Independence Rock.
"We've traveled near a thousand miles. This rock is our halfway
mark. We should have been here three weeks ago."

Mama leaned forward, her face reddening. "That's why
we're in no position to take chances. I want to continue on by
way of Fort Hall, the way we planned before we left Springfield."

The now-familiar tightness in my throat returned. Were my
parents going to argue again?

"It's only a possibility." Pa pulled off his hat, smoothed the
brim, then put it back on. "The men will have to vote on it.
Most of them haven't read this letter. I'll be passing it around
today."

"Puss!" Charlie, standing on the far side of our wagon circle
with five or six children, waved. "Are you coming with us? You
said you wanted to climb it." He pointed at the granite turtle.

Mama reached for her cup. "We stop too often for unnec-
essary things like rock climbing, James," she said. "That's why
we're three weeks behind."

"This rock is an exception, Margaret," Pa said, watching her rise. "It's a popular landmark. Hundreds of emigrants have carved their names on it."

"Everything is an exception." Mama shook out the rest of her coffee.

"I'm going with Charlie," I said, grateful for an excuse to leave.

"I'm going, too!" Patty scrambled up so quickly that she knocked over her bowl.

Tommy, who was feeding scraps of beef to little Cash, looked up. "I want to go! I want to go!" he shouted.

"You girls go on ahead," Pa said. "I'll keep Tommy busy here."

Mama set her lips in a tight line when I said, "We'll be back soon, promise."

Then Patty and I ran off.

We ascended Independence Rock's shallow ridges, Charlie turning to give us a hand up the gravelly parts. Pa was right about it being a popular landmark. The flow of westbound travelers—first explorers, then mountain men, and this year, whole families—had carved names and hopeful messages on its coarse surface, dating back twenty years.

I stopped on a flat ledge near the top, struck by the scene below, while the others climbed on. The seemingly endless green of the Great Plains had finally vanished behind us. But this landscape, with red outcrops casting morning shadows, was beautiful in its own way.

We'd passed other landmarks, but Independence Rock was the first I'd been allowed to climb. Courthouse Rock, at four hundred feet high, had looked like a real building from far away, and we could see it days before we reached it. Chimney

Rock was almost as tall, but no one could climb to the top because it ended in a steeple that pointed straight to heaven.

Now my eyes traced the westward meanderings of our next river, the Sweetwater. Pa told me we would follow it into a miles-wide valley that cut through the Rockies, called South Pass.

My gaze returned to the camp below. A breeze rippled the wagon covers, and though some party members were inside, I could see men making repairs and women huddled in conversation. Children ran about, stirring up coarse sand, their shrill voices drifting up to me. Hundreds of cattle grazed on clumps of sage outside the wagon circle. As big as the Russell Company was, from up here it looked small and defenseless.

It was a rare moment of solitude, and the troublesome thoughts I'd kept at bay for so long broke through.

When had I first suspected my father wasn't prepared for this journey? Was it the first time he and Mama argued about the Hastings Cutoff? Or before that, when party members blamed our oversized family wagon for slowing them down? Or was it even before *that*, in Independence, when Pa said we'd missed our meeting with Colonel Russell, and Mama looked so scared?

Only halfway. That meant we could still turn back, didn't it? For a moment I imagined us pulling up to our Springfield house and resuming our old lives. But that was impossible. Our house was sold. Grandma was gone. The girl who'd lived in that house was gone, too.

"I carved Patty's initials up here. Where do you want yours?" Charlie's call gave me a start, and I realized my eyes were filled with tears. Flushing, I blinked them away and pointed to the rock wall behind me. "Right here," I said, a bit too loudly. "But I want to carve them myself."

Charlie climbed down without comment, then held out a hand to Patty.

"Charlie," I said, "Do you think the rest of our journey will be as hard as the first part?"

"No doubt," he said as he helped Patty down. "We still have mountains to cross, Puss. Deserts, too."

My face must have fallen, because when he looked at me he quickly added, "But see all the names carved here? If these folks made it, so will we."

The other children climbed down to the ledge, and for the next hour or so we took turns carving. Charlie's sensible words lifted my spirits. Or maybe it was simply standing beside him that lifted my spirits. In any case, I pushed my worries to the back of my mind and scraped a big V and R on the hard surface. Ed Breen scratched out " E Breen." Charlie carved "C S, 1846," and we all laughed when he added "CAL or Bust!" beneath his initials.

Eleven

July 1846. The Vote.

Some of the party members found the sweeping sameness of the plains monotonous. Not me. I had the best rides of my life there with Billy, and I knew I'd never forget them. Still, the rugged grandeur of the Rockies was overwhelming.

Formidable summits dwarfed Pa and me as we rode side by side through South Pass. He estimated the flat valley to be at least twenty miles wide. "Don't expect the other mountain ranges to be this easy to cross," he said as we admired far-off peaks on either side. Last winter's snow still clung to their shadowed crevices. "None of them have passes this wide," he added. "Not that I've read about, anyway."

"What do you mean 'others'?" I asked, my eyes now on Charlie, who was riding ahead with Uncle George. "I thought the only other mountain range we have to cross is the Sierra."

"That's true if we take the longer route," Pa answered casually. He cleared his throat. "But if we take the Hastings Cutoff, we'll cross the Wasatch Range first."

That cutoff again. I started to question him, then immediately changed my mind. Best to think about something else.

Once through South Pass we set up camp near Little Sandy, a shallow river shaded by a single sparse willow. A half-mile ahead the Oregon Trail curved northwest while a narrower trail, the one that led to the Hastings Cutoff, forked off in a southwest direction.

Charlie claimed that on this side of the Rockies waters ran west instead of east, like we were all used to. I believed him, of course. Charlie knew all about that kind of thing. Still, I wanted to see for myself. So right after I brushed and watered Billy, Leanna and I walked toward Little Sandy's banks.

"You mean all the rivers and streams and creeks and"—Leanna searched for more words—"and everything else watery changes direction just because they're on the west side of the Rockies?" she asked as we left camp.

"That's what he says," I answered. "They flow toward the Pacific Ocean. And on the east side, they flow toward the Atlantic Ocean."

Leanna reached behind her neck for her long braid. She wound it around her fingers. "Even in the flat places?"

"Everywhere. Charlie calls this area here the Great Divide. Get it?"

"That sounds real crazy, Puss." Leanna flashed me a smile, clearly amused. "Ma never told us that, and she's a *teacher*." But she quickened her step to the banks.

Sure enough, Little Sandy flowed lazily toward the setting sun.

"See?" I said, a confusing pride in Charlie welling up in me.

Leanna laughed in astonishment. "Well, Puss, I guess your sweetheart is right again."

"Charlie? He's not my sweetheart!" My face caught fire. I bent down to pick up a rock so she wouldn't see. "Why did you say that?"

"It's the way you act around him." The laughter was gone from Leanna's voice. "Like he can't do or say anything wrong." She paused. "Don't worry, Puss. I won't tell anyone."

I gave her a sidelong glance, then tossed the rock and watched it splash. "He's too old, anyway," I said.

"He won't always be too old." Leanna skipped a stone all the way to the opposite bank. "Ma is twenty years younger than Papa, and they get along just fine."

When I said nothing, she asked, "What's the difference in your parents' ages?"

"I don't know," I lied. "I've never thought about it." I tossed another rock, farther this time. "Fourteen years," I finally said.

Campfire was over early that night—at least for the women and children. The men, Mama told us, were going to hold a meeting.

"We'll keep busy here in the wagon," she said, lifting the glass from the lamp, then striking a match to light the wick. A pool of light spread across the sofas and sleeping platforms, then up the canvas walls as Mama turned the lamp's wheel. I plunked down crossly next to Patty, who'd begun playing with the little doll Mr. Hardcoop had made her.

"It's not fair we can't be there," I said. Mama didn't answer.

"It's time to take a vote, boys," Pa's voice boomed outside. "We're little more than halfway to California. This cutoff will save us three hundred miles—maybe four hundred!"

With a barely audible sigh, Mama sat on the sofa across from us and took up her embroidery hoop. "Finish your folding, Puss," she said, nodding at the laundry bag.

I exchanged a quick glance with Patty, then pulled a shirt onto my lap, folded it, and slapped it on a pile that I'd started before supper. Why did Mama make us fold clothes before stuffing them back in the bag? No one else folded their clothes on the trail, not even the Donners.

Pa's voice continued, "Most other companies have passed us by."

"You don't say," said another man, his voice tinged with sarcasm.

I stopped midfold, recognizing Mr. Keseberg's accent. "And vy do you think dat *is*, James Reed? Could it be a particular vagon dat's causing the problem?"

Patty was trying to fit a tiny nightcap over her doll's painted hair. "That Mr. Keseberg is the meanest man I've ever—"

"Hush." I pulled another shirt from the basket. Mama's eyes stayed on her needlework.

"Listen to this, boys," Pa said. "Hastings describes the cut-off clearly." I imagined him paging through Hastings' yellow-covered book.

> "The most direct route, for the California emigrants, would be to leave the Oregon route, about two hundred miles east from Fort Hall; thence bearing west southwest, to the Salt Lake; and thence continuing down to the bay of St. Francisco."

"Ve won't find our vay with *dose* directions!" Mr. Keseberg shot back. There was a rumbling of voices and some laughter.

"Mama," Tommy called from our bed. "Will you tell me a story?"

"Hush, Tommy. Go to sleep."

"I'll tell you one," Patty said. She laid down her doll and climbed up to the bed.

"How do we know we won't get lost?" another voice asked.

I couldn't bear to just listen anymore. I drew the canvas flap aside. Silhouettes of twenty or thirty men surrounded the glow of the campfire like strings of unmatched paper dolls. Pa was standing a bit above them on a split log. The flames lit his face, and I could see the hint of a smile beneath his beard.

"Have you forgotten this?" He waved a piece of crinkled paper over his head. "The letter Mr. Bonney showed us at Independence Rock? His dark eyes scanned the faces of his listeners. "Our guide across the cutoff will be none other than Hastings himself!"

Again a rumbling of voices, but this time with a different tone. Pa held up his hand. The voices lowered then, and I could no longer make out their words.

I closed the flap and turned to Mama. "I think they're going to take a vote."

Her shoulders sagged.

Within the hour Pa was leaning through the door, telling us what we already suspected. We, the Donners, and a few other families would take the Hastings Cutoff by way of Fort Bridger, then join the California Trail. The rest of the party would take the longer route to the California Trail.

"How many are coming with us?" I asked uneasily, stuffing the last of the clothing into a canvas bag.

Pa was watching Mama. She hadn't looked up from her needlework. "Oh, including children and teamsters—eighty, maybe ninety. The Eddys, the Murphys, the Kesebergs, and another German family." He turned to me. "And the Breens have decided to come along, after all."

The Breens were coming with us! A wave of happiness washed over me. Maybe I would never be a Catholic, but at least I'd get the chance to hear more Catholic prayers. Maybe memorize them.

"George Donner was just elected our new captain," Pa added. His mouth twitched when he said it, and I realized he was disappointed.

Pa was the logical choice. From the time we left Springfield, he'd been the decision maker for the three families. Even after we joined the bigger company, Colonel Russell often asked Pa's advice. Yet there was no denying Uncle George, with his mild, easygoing manner, was better liked among the men.

"It should have been you, Pa," Patty said from the bed. "You're the one who always knows what to do."

"Oh, it's fine with me, Patty. It's enough that our friends are taking the cutoff with us."

Patty lowered her voice. "Mr. Keseberg's not our friend."

Mama stood up then, unsmiling but surprisingly calm. "Well, James, at least it's finally settled."

Pa's expression softened. He stepped through the door and hugged Mama as though he would never stop. Then he smiled at Patty and me over her shoulder.

"Time for sleep now. We leave early tomorrow."

TWELVE

July 1846. The Cutoff.

Several days later our newly named Donner Party of twenty wagons arrived in a lush meadow bordered by rugged cliffs. Even though I'd been told not to expect a bustling community like Fort Laramie, I wilted inside when I caught my first glimpse of Fort Bridger. The tiny supply post was made up of two log cabins joined by a long, fenced-in corral, housing livestock.

"They say Mr. Bridger was a trapper at one time," Pa told me as we rode through a low, open gate. "He built this post last year for people taking the Hastings Cutoff. It's our last place for supplies until we reach Sutter's Fort."

Really? The last place? Sutter's Fort, I knew, was in California. And California was at least seven hundred miles away. Wait. Not anymore. Pa had said it would be closer to four hundred, now that we were taking the cutoff.

It may have been small, but Fort Bridger was the first hint of civilization we'd seen since we left Fort Laramie a month earlier. At least we could drop off letters in hopes that someone traveling east would deliver them, replenish our dwindling food supplies, replace livestock that had disappeared on the trail, and make wagon repairs before starting out on the last leg of our journey.

And here we would meet Lansford Hastings, author of *The Emigrants' Guide to Oregon and California*—the man who would lead us safely through the cutoff he'd named for himself.

"That's strange," Pa said as he dismounted Glaucus.

"What's strange?"

Pa made a full turn, surveying the meadow. "Not many people here. I expected more."

An Indian in white men's clothing tended a horse in the corral. A trapper, small gray pelts slung over his shoulder, disappeared through the door of one of the cabins. Two men in sombreros sat at a low table on the porch, playing cards.

Our wagon train formed a circle in the tall grass. Children drifted to a stream that ran nearby, and I listened to their splashing and laughter as I pulled off Billy's saddle and led him beyond the circle to graze. Milt and Charlie picked up shotguns and walked toward low hills, most likely hoping to bring back small game for supper. Pa and Uncle George headed toward the cabins in search of Mr. Hastings.

I'd just begun to brush Billy when I saw Pa and Uncle George walking back toward the wagons. They were alone, and something indefinable in Pa's bearing alarmed me.

"Where's Hastings?" I heard Mr. Breen ask them.

"*Gone!*" Uncle George barked.

What? This couldn't be happening again. I dropped the brush and ran to the palace car, where people were already gathering.

Uncle George's usually pleasant expression had soured. I looked from his scowl to Pa's stunned appearance.

"Now, wait just a minute." Mr. Breen's tenor voice rose a notch. "That letter said Hastings was goin' to lead a wagon train through the cutoff."

Mama came up behind me and laid her hands on my shoulders.

"He did, Patrick." Pa removed his hat, ran his fingers through his hair, then put it back on. "He led a company of sixty-six wagons out of here a few days back. He told Mr. Bridger we can follow his tracks."

Mr. Keseberg's ice-blue eyes froze on Pa. He gestured toward the mountains. "Ve're going through dat mess with no guide? Ve voted to take da cutoff on your assurance Hastings would lead us."

Oh, this was so unfair! Mr. Keseberg was acting as though it was Pa's fault Lansford Hastings had left without us. Mama's grip on my shoulders tightened.

Uncle George looked from Mr. Keseberg to Pa, and apparently decided to take Pa's side. The harshness in his voice relaxed. "We've come this far on our own, folks. We can do the same now."

"We've been deceived."

Everyone turned. Aunt Tamsen was standing at the edge of the crowd, arms folded across her chest, looking every bit the stern schoolteacher. "I knew something like this would happen, George. You men put far too much trust in this Hastings character. None of you have even *met* the man."

"Now dear..." Uncle George's face reddened and his voice trailed off.

I held my breath, watching for Pa's reaction to Aunt Tamsen's statement. Even if he agreed we'd somehow been deceived, I was sure he'd never admit it.

Pa took off his hat again and slapped it against his leg, as though to shake off more trail dust. "We'll be fine, Tamsen," he said irritably. "Bridger says the trail through the mountains is well marked. It'll take no more than a week to get through."

Uncle George chimed in, avoiding his wife's gaze. "Bridger admits the Salt Desert crossing will be difficult. It's a forty-mile stretch, but he says we can cross it in two days."

Grownups' voices swirled around me—angry, accusing, re-assuring—and I withdrew into my own thoughts. It *was* scary Mr. Hastings had left without us, but then again, he was leading sixty-six wagons. So that had to mean that Pa's friend Mr. Clyman was wrong back at Fort Laramie, didn't it? Wagons *could* make it through the Wasatch.

What did Charlie think about all this? I searched for his face in the crowd, then remembered he'd gone off hunting with Milt. If only he were here. He might say something sensible and encouraging. He might calm everyone.

Mr. Breen's thickening brogue pushed through my thoughts. "We should move on soon as possible," he said. "Tomorrow mornin'. Or the next, latest."

But we let the tired oxen graze another three days to gain strength. Some of the men used the time to repair axles and wagon wheels. Others bought more livestock. One of Mr. Bridger's workers was a blacksmith, and Glaucus and Billy got new horseshoes.

The fresh buffalo meat we'd enjoyed on the plains was a memory now, and we all had to go back to eating ordinary pioneer food. Mama bought new supplies of dried beans and flour, cornmeal, sugar, and coffee. Patty and I helped her pack them in the kitchen wagon.

New members joined us at Fort Bridger. A man named Mr. McCutchen, traveling with his wife and baby, had been stranded at the fort for days with a broken-down wagon he couldn't afford to fix. Mr. Breen helped the young father repair the axles, and Pa and the Donner brothers chipped in to buy new wheels. Mr. McCutchen was "strong as an ox," according to Pa. The men nicknamed him Big Bill.

Leanna's parents took on another stranded traveler, a young, horseless invalid named Luke Hallorhan. He'd developed a bad cough, and when he became too weak to walk, his party had cruelly abandoned him.

"Ma says it's consumption," Leanna told me later at campfire. She confided she'd been washing Luke's face that evening, and he'd awakened long enough to tell her she had pretty eyes.

"Puss, he's so thin. I wish we knew more about him. He's too sick to talk much."

I scooted closer to her for warmth. "Do you think he'll be all right?"

"Ma thinks so. But he told her if anything happens to him, he wants to leave her and Papa all of his worldly goods." Leanna shook her head. "It's so sad. He has nothing but that little suitcase."

"It'll be hard to for him to get well while we're traveling," I said, thinking of Grandma.

Leanna nodded. "Ma says he'd be better off settled down in one place, but she won't leave him here. She says she doesn't trust Mr. Bridger any more than she trusts Lansford Hastings."

But Pa and Uncle George trusted Mr. Bridger. Each evening the grizzled, soft-spoken old man walked from his cabin to the Donner camp to reassure them our party could safely follow Hastings' tracks. One night, with Tommy asleep beside me, I heard them talking long into the night about California's future, and something called Manifest Destiny.

I asked Pa about it the next morning over breakfast.

"Manifest Destiny means that God intends for the United States to spread all the way to the Pacific Ocean," he explained, pouring coffee into his metal cup. "That's why I keep telling you that California won't always belong to Mexico. It will be ours one day." He winked at me over the rim. "And the most enterprising of us will already be there when it happens."

Then he showed me a letter he was writing to Uncle Jim, describing Mr. Bridger and his partner as "two very excellent and accommodating gentlemen." He read aloud:

> "The rest of the Californians went the long route— feeling afraid of Hastings' Cutoff. Mr. Bridger informs me that the route we design to take is a fine level road, with plenty of water and grass..."

Thirteen

August 1846. Another Death.

We left Fort Bridger on the first day of August. The cut-off trail wasn't as level as Mr. Bridger described, but Pa said it was no bumpier than some we'd been on before. He and I rode in front, following Hastings' wagon tracks over rocky ridges and through wide ravines toward the Wasatch Mountains. On the seventh day we followed a creek to the mouth of a narrow canyon bordered by red cliffs.

Pa reined in Glaucus and admired how the deep greens of the pines lightened as they grew from the canyon floor to the tree line. "I've read about this place. It's the entrance to Weber Canyon." His voice was edged with excitement. "We'll follow it all the way through the Wasatch to the Salt Lake Valley."

"Vat's *dat?*" A deep voice boomed behind us, and I turned in the saddle. Mr. Keseberg had caught up to us. Frowning, he pointed to a large piece of paper clearly propped in a nearby bush, a branch stabbed through its center.

"We—we didn't see—" I stammered. Pa dismounted.

Mr. Keseberg leaned down from his horse and snatched it up. "It's a note," he said reproachfully as he unfolded it.

I watched his cold eyes flick back and forth as he read. My insides clenched when I saw them narrow.

"Hastings says here ve shouldn't go by way of Weber Canyon. His party is still struggling to get through. He vants someone to fetch him, and he'll lead us through a better route."

Mr. Keseberg's face blazed crimson. He crumpled the note and threw it at Pa's feet. "Hastings has promoted this cutoff for more than a year," he yelled. "Vat does this mean, James Reed?"

Pa stepped back as though physically shoved. He picked up the note and began reading. In the moments that followed, others arrived, and word of its contents traveled from wagon to wagon. I looked from Mr. Breen's frightened expression, to Aunt Tamsen's I-told-you-so shake of the head, to Mama's bewildered silence. Mr. Clyman's warning—"Anything can happen out there. Anything."—ran through my head as party members pummeled Pa with questions he couldn't possibly answer. Why hadn't Hastings known that wagons couldn't get through the canyon? Did this mean Mr. Clyman had told the truth about the cutoff back at Fort Laramie, and that Hastings had lied about it in his book? Had Mr. Bridger lied to us as well, or had Hastings fooled him, too? And what about this other route Hastings now wanted us to take? How could we trust it was any better?

Pa held up his hands. "I'll go after Hastings. I'll bring him back." His voice was loud and steady, but when I saw how white he was I pinched the inside of my arm to keep the tears back.

"Go *now*, James," Mr. Breen pleaded. "We can't afford to wait."

Then everything happened too fast to follow. Big Bill volunteered to go with Pa. Charlie said he'd go, too. Within a dizzying half hour, the three men had packed a few supplies and were saying their good-byes.

Pa's face was expressionless. He gave all of us children distracted hugs. "Help your mother out," was all he said.

I tried not to give in to the hollowness inside as Pa mounted Glaucus. Instinctively, I dug my hand into my pocket for my rosary necklace before remembering I had packed it away. I squeezed my eyes shut. *Protect them. Please.* When I opened them, the men were already disappearing into the canyon. Charlie was last; his flat hat melted into the shadows.

Patty peppered Mama with tearful questions and, as if on cue, Tommy suddenly tried to bolt after Pa. Mama, tight-lipped and pale, held him back by the collar.

"He'll be back before you know it," she assured us.

We could only wait. We set up camp with the Donners and Breens at the mouth of the canyon. Other party members spread out along the narrow creek bed, settling into the sandy areas between rocks and brush. One day went by, then two. Mama stayed busy by catching up with mending and needlework. Milt tended the animals and hunted small game with the other teamsters. Two of the Breen boys caught and killed a huge rattlesnake. Tommy and the little Donner boys splashed in the shallow waters for relief from the heat. Patty and I picked wild blackberries with the Donner girls or played fetch with little Cash.

On the fourth afternoon three wagons appeared from the direction of Fort Bridger. I was rummaging through our supply wagon, trying to find another book to read to Tommy, when I heard unfamiliar voices raised in greeting. I stuck my head out the flap.

A florid-faced, pot-bellied man was introducing himself to Uncle George. "I hear you're the party captain, sir," he said solemnly. "I'm William Graves." He explained his large family and his teamster were trying to get to California. Mama and the Donners welcomed them, and the new party members set up camp near us.

I couldn't help but notice the Graveses' teamster's dark good looks and flirtatious manner. Leanna giggled nervously when he nodded and smiled in our direction.

"I found out his name. It's John Snyder," she whispered to me that night at campfire. The amiable young man had pulled out a banjo and was encouraging us all to join him in song.

"But don't pin your hopes on him, Puss," she teased. "He's sweet on one of Mr. Graves's daughters. That pretty one, over there. Her name's Mary."

I followed Leanna's nod. A doe-eyed girl with wavy hair sat on a blanket near our teamster, Milt. Maybe it was just the firelight—her face glowed as John Snyder performed. But it was Milt's expression that held my attention. He watched Mary Graves as though entranced, a half smile upon his lips. For the first time I understood what Grandma's old expression, "wearing his heart on his sleeve," meant. Poor shy, awkward Milt. He'd never had a sweetheart, and now he was smitten by someone already spoken for.

Pa rode into camp alone and exhausted the next afternoon. I was picking berries in the canyon with Leanna, and I called out to Mama excitedly before running to greet him. Anxious party members surrounded him before he could dismount.

"First of all, Big Bill and Charlie are all right," he said, finding Mrs. McCutchen's frightened face in the crowd. "Their horses gave out, is all. They're camping with Hastings' company." Dark hollows circled Pa's eyes. "They'll be back as soon as the horses gain strength, probably day after tomorrow."

Mr. Keseberg pushed to the front of the crowd, his face flushed. "But vere's Hastings?" he demanded.

Pa didn't answer. He climbed down from a small brown horse to hug Mama, who'd worked her way through.

"Pa, what happened to Glaucus?" I whispered as I took the reins.

"She's resting up, too. Mr. Hastings gave me this horse."

I searched Pa's weary face, alarmed. Was the trail so bad that even Glaucus gave out?

"I *said*, vere's Hastings, Reed?" Mr. Keseberg's voice was harsher this time.

Pa sank down heavily on the palace car steps. "We need a meeting, boys." He took off his hat and wiped his arm across his forehead. Mama urged him to eat, but he shook his head. More party members gathered, their faces full of questions.

"Weber Canyon is impassable by wagon," Pa finally said. "It's choked with trees and boulders." He paused for the crowd's reaction, but they were stonily silent, waiting for more.

Hastings' company, he continued, chopped down trees and hacked their way through the brush to widen the trail. They made a pulley of rope and tackle to lower all sixty-six wagons, one by one, down a high ridge. Even so, one wagon slipped out and fell to the bottom of a canyon. No one was in it, but the family lost everything they owned.

"They did make it through, but cattle were lost and wagons were damaged. By the time we found them, they were camped in the Salt Lake Valley." Pa paused again. A shadow crossed his face and he added quietly, "Hastings isn't coming back for us."

His words were met with groans of dismay and some cursing.

"But he *promised* he'd come back!" a tearful voice cried out. Mama reached out and squeezed my shoulder. The voice had been mine. I bit my lip and looked down at my feet.

Pa's voice continued, "He led me up a peak and pointed out another route, the one I took back here. I notched the trees to blaze a trail. We can follow it out."

"'Is it any better than the first route?" Mr. Breen wiped his freckled brow with his striped handkerchief. He looked as tired as Pa, even though he'd been waiting at camp with the rest of us.

Both routes, Pa admitted, were difficult. Although Hastings' company had widened the path on the first route, it was longer, and it had that high ridge. The second route was shorter, but we would have to cut our own path to get the wagons through.

"Even so, I think that's the one we should take," Pa said, standing. "We can get the wagons over the ridge without using a pulley."

"But do we have enough man-power to clear a trail?" Uncle George asked. "Hastings has a lot more able-bodied men than we do. Maybe we should stick to the route that's already been cleared."

The tense discussion went back and forth for another hour. I waited with the women and children while the men tried to decide which route to take. In the end, they agreed on Pa's choice, the shorter one.

The next morning most of the men and older boys, carrying hatchets, picks, and shovels, disappeared into the aspen-choked canyon. They trudged back at sunset with bruised arms, blistered hands, and discouraging stories. They had chopped down trees and dragged them clear. They had attacked thorny thickets with their bare hands. They had used shovels and brute strength to move boulders.

They had cleared only two miles.

"They argue more than they work," Pa complained that night over supper. I was surprised to hear him say such a thing; it wasn't like Pa to speak discouragingly in front of us children. "George Donner doesn't act like a captain. He lets them get away with it."

Day after day, the strenuous work went on. Pa let it be known he didn't think certain men were working hard enough. One afternoon a Donner teamster stalked into camp, refusing to go back to work. "I don't take orders from James Reed," he declared.

Another night at supper, Pa told us that Mr. Graves's teamster, John Snyder, had a bad temper.

"Why, I can't imagine that handsome young man being anything but pleasant," Mama said.

"Oh, he's real nice, Pa," I agreed. "Everyone likes John Snyder."

Pa shook his head. "He can't handle frustration. Today he hurled his shovel when he got angry. It narrowly missed Milt. I had to put that young man in his place."

I squirmed uncomfortably, wondering what my father had said to the popular teamster.

Charlie and Big Bill still hadn't returned, and a rumor went around camp that the two men had gone on with Hastings' company, abandoning the rest of us. Of course I didn't believe a word of it, but each day my eyes searched the mountains for Charlie. Where was he?

It took a week of chopping, dragging, and forcing our wagons along the roughly cleared trail a few miles at a time to get us halfway up a low ridge. My family spent an entire afternoon there; the palace car fell over while being pulled to the top by four yoke of oxen. The other families waited unhappily while Pa, Milt, and Uncle George partially unpacked it, righted it, and then packed it up again.

But that evening when we descended into a sparse meadow I heard those ahead of us shouting out greetings. I was so relieved at what I saw that a cry escaped me, and I clapped my hand over my mouth. There was Charlie, sitting against a boulder next to Big Bill McCutchen. Glaucus and the men's own two horses stood nearby.

"We haven't eaten for days," was the first thing Big Bill said when his wife ran up to him.

"You stay with your husband, lass. I'll take care of 'em." Mrs. Breen hurried back to her wagons for food. More people gathered to greet the two men. By then I'd become uneasy about Charlie's blank expression.

"What's wrong with Charlie?" I whispered to Pa.

Pa shook his head.

"Charlie," I called out. "Are you all right?"

Charlie lifted his chin and nodded, but his eyes looked right through me.

Shaken, I hung back, sneaking glances at Charlie while Pa examined Glaucus. Big Bill described how he and Charlie became lost on their way back to camp. They rode the mountains on horseback for days, he said, leading Glaucus behind them. Too exhausted to go farther, they had given up by the time they reached the meadow.

Mrs. Breen arrived with bread and dried meat.

"We were about to eat one of the horses," Big Bill told her, holding out his hands gratefully.

"Oh, but—you wouldn't eat Glaucus," I exclaimed.

Charlie didn't seem to hear me. He held out his hands to Mrs. Breen, his expression unchanged.

"That's enough, Puss," Pa said softly.

"Pa," I whispered again, "What's wrong with them?"

Big Bill wolfed down a chunk of meat. "We would have eaten *anything*," he said.

"Pa—" I tugged at my father's sleeve.

"*Virginia*. I said that's enough."

Three days later we finally set foot on the Salt Lake Valley. Charlie had recovered by then—he had no memory of the day we found him and Big Bill—and I had pushed the disturbing incident from my mind.

The terrain ahead of us was flat as the plains, though here the earth was reddish brown, with occasional low mountains breaking through its surface. This is where Pa had found Hastings and his company. They were long gone now, but everyone was too exhausted to care. It had taken a full eighteen days to hack our way through thirty miles of the Wasatch.

I looked at the wide-open flatness and thought that the worst was surely over. Moving ahead would be so much easier—faster, too. Maybe the party's unfair anger toward Pa would fade away.

We set up evening camp near a freshwater spring. A cooling breeze wafted in from the west. Men unhitched the oxen and women started campfires. Pa and I were standing outside the wagon circle grooming Glaucus and Billy when Uncle George approached us.

"I have bad news," he said. "Young Mr. Hallorhan just died."

His words were so unexpected that it took me a dizzying moment to grasp their meaning. "But—I thought Luke was getting better."

Pa gave me a sympathetic glance. He was about to speak when Uncle George opened his hand to reveal a silver medal. "Look what I found in that suitcase of his, James."

Pa took the medal and studied it solemnly. "Luke was a Master Mason?" he asked, turning it over. "Who would have thought?"

I recognized the medal. Pa had a similar one, and he was mighty proud of it. He belonged to a men's organization called the Masons. I didn't know much about it, except that it had members all over the world, and some of its rituals were secret. Pa had once explained his relationship to other members. "Masons are brothers for life, Puss," he said. "We're obligated to help each other in times of trouble."

Uncle George spoke again. "That's not all. There was fifteen hundred dollars in that suitcase of his."

Pa's eyes widened. *"Fifteen hundred dollars!* And we thought he was just some poor waif."

Uncle George shook his head. "What do we really know about people we meet on the trail? He never had a chance to tell us his dreams for California."

Pity for Luke and something else—a wave of dread—swept through me. The worst was *not* over. Anything could happen out here. Anything. I ran back to the palace car.

"Oh. But he was so young," Mama said when I told her what happened. She held me close. "Another death."

Luke was a stranger to us. Most everyone wanted to bury him quickly and hurry on the next morning, but Pa made up his mind to hold a Masonic service, and there was no changing it. The party unwillingly camped an extra day while Milt and Charlie built Luke a crude coffin from spare wagon planks. Pa spent hours looking for a perfect gravesite.

That evening I held hands with Leanna as our two families buried Luke a mile from camp near a lone, bristly pine. Pa was doing right by his Masonic brother, but other party members were angry. Lost days had turned into lost weeks, food supplies were dwindling, and no one knew how much longer it would take to reach California.

The resentment surrounding Luke's service was a startling contrast from the support surrounding Grandma's back in Alcove Spring, when we thought we had plenty of time to reach California. Even our friends the Breens pointedly stayed away. Were they turning against Pa too? While he droned the long Masonic ritual, I whispered a line I remembered from listening to Mr. Breen recite the Rosary that long-ago night at Fort Laramie.

"Holy Mary, Mother of God, pray for us sinners, now and at the hour of our death."

FOURTEEN

September 1846. The Great Salt Desert.

Over the next few days we followed Lansford Hastings' tracks over a scrubby plain south of the Great Salt Lake. The blue-white sky was cloudless, and the mercury in Pa's thermometer rose to the high nineties. The next section of the Hastings Cutoff—the Great Salt Desert—lay ahead.

"The Salt Desert is full of a mineral salt called alkali," Charlie told me as the two of us rode side by side in front of the wagons. Pa had gone on ahead to scout our next campsite.

"It kills everything," he continued, knitting his brows above the rim of his glasses. "Not even cactus or scrub brush can grow in salt."

What could be more barren than what we were riding through now? I wondered. The surrounding emptiness reflected the spirits of the entire party. Few spoke as they rode or walked beside the travel-worn wagons. Even the children were quiet. The oxen, drained from their ordeal in the mountains, pulled their loads silently. Only a few dogs, following along behind, occasionally yipped and whined.

I stroked Billy's neck, then leaned forward and ran my hand down his chest. He still carried his rider dutifully, but was weakened by our trek through the Wasatch. I could feel the ribs beneath his once-sleek coat.

"Puss!"

Pa was galloping toward us, waving his hat in the air. "I found springs and plenty of grass a few hours up," he shouted. "Go tell your mother and the others."

Glad to be the bearer of good news, I turned Billy and sped back to the wagons. By early evening we were setting up camp in a grassy valley wedged between two low hills.

"I know Bridger said the Salt Desert would take two days and a night to cross, but I don't know who to believe anymore," I overheard Pa admit to Milt as the two men unhitched the oxen. "We've got to figure out a way to carry more water, just in case."

I'd been unable to shake the feeling of dread that had swept through me when Luke died, and its grip tightened with Pa's worried tone. I pondered our newest difficulty as I removed Billy's bridle and saddle outside the wagon circle. Lack of water had never been a problem before now. From the time we left Springfield, we'd always traveled near a river. I sent Billy off to graze, then shoved his saddle and bridle beneath the palace car. What if we ran out of water in the Salt Desert? What if we got thirsty?

"Patty!" I called out. "Let's get buckets and walk to the spring."

There would be no spare water for boiling during the crossing, so the women cooked and stored bacon and beans. The teamsters cut and bundled grass. Uncle George walked from family to family, quietly encouraging everyone to unload items. When he got to us, he looked pointedly at the palace car. "The lighter our wagons, the more water we can carry," he said firmly. "The oxen can't go without water for more than a few hours at a time, and if they don't make it across, none of us do."

Mama tearfully agreed to remove two boxes—one stuffed with linens, the other with raw fabric—from the palace car. Pa reluctantly removed a pull plow from the supply wagon.

Hours later I was still awake, Uncle George's warning echoing in my mind. The camp was eerily silent—not a voice or a bark or a flutter of wind outside. My mind drifted back longingly to the rippling green of the plains, where I spurred Billy on each day, and Leanna and I watched the older girls and boys dance in the firelight each night. Then it drifted farther back, to our house in Springfield, where Mary came over to ride Billy, and Grandma napped upstairs. I whispered the Lord's Prayer for comfort before falling into a fitful sleep.

We set off at sunrise, Pa and me in the lead. The meadow, now stripped of grass and oddly sprinkled with trunks, furniture, and farm equipment, faded behind us, and the shimmering landscape came into full view.

It looked like a blanket of snow in bright sunshine. Pa pointed out the scattered, shadowy mountains that broke through its white surface. The highest of them, Pilot Peak, was our destination. According to Hastings' book, Pilot Peak marked the other side of the forty-mile-wide crossing. Clear springs were said to bubble at its base.

As I bent to whisper encouragement to Billy, I noticed a board lying next to Hastings' wagon tracks. Pieces of tattered paper were clinging to it. "Pa," I said. "Someone's sign got knocked over."

Pa dismounted and leaned over for a closer look while I surveyed our surroundings. Scores more of the white scraps were scattered on the ground or caught on sagebrush.

Charlie caught up with us, and within a few more minutes nearly everyone was gathered around, staring at the fallen sign as though it were a snake in the sand, coiled and ready to strike.

"It must be a message for us," Charlie said, his voice quieter than usual.

"I don't know what it is," Pa answered. "This paper was attached to the sign. Birds must have torn it apart."

"Gather up scraps, everyone," Aunt Tamsen ordered, kneeling next to Pa. "If it is a message, I'm going to try to make sense of it." She smoothed the pieces still attached to the board.

We all scattered, looking for bits of paper caught in sagebrush and bringing them to the schoolteacher to puzzle together.

Mr. Keseberg crouched beside Aunt Tamsen as she worked. He bit his fleshy bottom lip as the words began to take form. "It's another note from Hastings," he said. "I recognize the writing."

Pa and I leaned closer as Aunt Tamsen eventually pieced enough scraps together to reveal a partial message. "Two days… two nights…hard driving…cross desert…reach water," she read aloud.

"Dat makes no sense," Mr. Keseberg spat, rising.

The grownups discussed what the partial message might mean. Mr. Bridger had said the journey would take two days and only *one* night. Was Hastings now telling us the desert went on for more than forty miles? Or did it mean it couldn't be traveled at our best pace of fifteen miles a day? More grownups raised their voices, and I couldn't help but notice the frightened faces of the smaller children as they watched their parents argue.

Pa's voice broke through the others. "I don't know what it means any more than you do," he said, staring out at the vastness that stretched before us. "But I *do* know we're wasting time standing here."

Aunt Tamsen stood, and the grownups gave up trying to make sense of the message. The sun was hanging directly above us when we stepped onto the white glitter.

It didn't take long to understand why traveling over a flat surface could take so long. Glue-like mud lurked beneath the thick salt crust, tugging at the wagon wheels whenever they broke through. The oxen strained with each step.

And the sun, I thought as Pa and I rode beside the palace car, must be hotter here than anywhere in the world. Salty sweat collected beneath the bonnet Grandma made me. It ran down my forehead and over my lips. My mouth was dry as cotton, but I knew better than to ask for water. More than a few children were already crying of thirst, and their mothers were close to tears with frustration.

Yet now and then pools of water appeared ahead of us—only to vanish into the salt as we got closer. I asked Pa about the unsettling images.

"Mirages," he explained. "Tricks of the eye in the desert."

Mama walked alongside Milt and the oxen while Patty and Tommy stayed in the wagon. "We'll have some a little later," she called back to them firmly when they called out for water. She ended up asking me to give them lumps of sugar to suck on. I took one, too.

The burnt-orange sun was melting into the desert floor when we stopped to water the livestock. Our oxen drank greedily from buckets, and our horses devoured the unbundled grass. I served Patty and Tommy cold beans and bacon. Mama doled out small rations of water. Then we rested inside the stifling palace car.

Pa returned from a hasty meeting with Uncle George and the other men. "We're starting out again in a half hour," he said.

Good, I thought. Night travel would be cooler. It was twilight, and the first stars had already appeared. Mama climbed into bed with the children, but she said I could ride through the night. Charlie, who'd been helping out with a weakening Uncle Jake, joined us too. I snuck Billy an extra bit of water before we started out again.

Soon after the sun set, the air turned cool and wind gusted down from the north, stirring up clouds of salt that stung my face. I rode close behind Pa and Charlie. They were following Hastings' wagon tracks in the light of a full moon, silent, heads bent. From time to time, I turned around to see Milt, hat pulled low, trudging next to the palace car.

Before long it was so cold that Pa made me wear his heavy jacket. I pulled the collar over my nose and mouth and watched the moon set behind a low mountain. Uncaring stars glowed overhead. Billy's hooves crunched through the brittle salt.

"There's nothing here to hold the heat in," I heard Charlie say to Pa. "Not a living thing."

Those with lighter loads, like the Kesebergs and Breens, pulled ahead and disappeared. The Donner families moved more slowly, but eventually crept ahead of our wagons. By the time I finally gave into exhaustion and went to bed, they too were out of sight.

"Where is everyone?" My heart dropped when I looked through the door of the palace car the next morning. Our three wagons stood alone in the whiteness. Pilot Peak appeared no closer than when we started out.

"They've gone on ahead," Pa answered without looking up. He and Milt sat at the camp stove, heads bent over their reheated beans.

Were we in trouble? I tried to read Pa's expression for a clue, but his eyes stayed on his plate. He seemed intent on eating.

"It's every family for itself, Puss," Mama said, dishing up a plate for me. Her movements were quick, angry. "Sit down and eat something. Then we'll get Patty and Tommy up."

"And Charlie?" I asked, stepping down.

Mama cocked her head in the direction of the vanished wagons. "He's up ahead with the Donners."

I sat down with a thud. Best not to ask any more questions.

When we started moving again I didn't have the heart to climb back on poor Billy. I stroked his neck and took hold of his reins. Mama and Patty walked beside me, our eyes trained on Pilot Peak. Tommy lay listlessly with little Cash on our bed inside the palace car.

At some point that day Patty called out, "Over there! More wagons!" We turned and peered through heat waves rising from the white shimmer. Halfway between us and the northern horizon, three wagons headed west. One man rode ahead on horseback, and spare horses and cattle trailed behind. Three women and a pony walked next to the lead wagon.

Pa had already spotted them. He raised his hand in greeting. The man riding in front of the wagons raised his hand at the same time.

"I wonder why they're so far off the trail," Mama said. She added in a puzzled tone, "Their lead wagon looks nearly as big as our palace car."

I waved just as the girl beside a pony waved back. Milt waved both arms over his head in unison with a rider in the other wagon company.

"They're our mirror images," he said wonderingly. "Even the horses are identical."

A slow chill ran down my spine. "You mean they're *us*?"

"Don't look. Don't look!" Mama's voice trembled. "They aren't real. They're a mirage."

No one said a word after that. We continued to trudge through the heat, sneaking uneasy glances at our ghostly doubles until they vanished in the midday glare.

"It's obvious this desert is a lot more than forty miles across," Pa said the next morning. It was already hot and we were standing in the western shadow of the palace car. Pa crossed his arms and squinted at Pilot Peak as though to will it closer. "We're going to need more water before we reach the spring." He dropped his arms. "I'm going on ahead to bring some back."

"I don't believe this, James!" Mama's angry voice caused all three of us children to flinch. "You're going to leave your family out here alone?"

Pa raised his hands and shook his head, "I don't want to hear it, Margaret. We need water. I can ride there and back in a matter of hours."

The sternness in his voice frightened me. Mama said nothing more, but set her lips in an angry line.

"Milt," he continued, "Keep the oxen yoked and drive them as far as they'll go." And with that he rode off on Glaucus, leaving us behind in the blistering heat.

We had no choice but to keep moving. Patty and Tommy stayed in the palace car with little Cash. I led Billy and walked beside Mama. She barely spoke; I knew she was fuming inside. The heat from the salt floor rose through my thick leather boots. I licked my lips; they were blistered and peeling. Our progress was excruciatingly slow. Shortly after noon Milt brought the wagons to a halt and unhitched all sixteen of our oxen.

The poor creatures' bony hindquarters and shrunken chests made their big heads look heavier than ever.

"I'm driving them on ahead to the spring, Mrs. Reed," Milt announced. "The horses, too. These animals will die if they aren't watered soon."

Mama didn't argue. She knew she had no say. And although I didn't like the idea of Billy leaving my side, I knew Milt was right.

Now we were truly alone—Mama, Patty, Tommy and me. It was too hot to do anything but sit inside the sweltering wagon and wait for the men. I tried not to think about how dangerous our situation was, especially when we drank nearly the last of our water. Mama and I told stories to keep Patty and Tommy distracted, and eventually the sun set on our teamless wagons. Still later, a cold chill settled over us. It was our third night on the desert.

Patty and Tommy finally fell asleep beside me. Mama was silent in the other bed, but I was certain she was still awake, probably praying. I thought about the mirage we'd seen yesterday. What was that ghostly family doing out here? What were *we* doing out here? Were we going to vanish into the desert, too?

Never had I felt so abandoned. I closed my eyes and remembered sitting in the pew of the Catholic Church, feeling God's presence inside me. I tried to feel it in this unholy place, but nothing happened. Maybe I needed to be holding the rosary necklace to feel it.

Or maybe God had abandoned us, too.

I awoke to the sound of Pa's voice. He was telling Mama it had taken him eight hours to ride to Pilot Peak and back.

I bolted out of bed and nearly fell from the platform. "Pa!"

"Oh, James," Mama said dejectedly. "Four hours by horseback. Then it'll be at least another day by wagon."

I scrambled from the palace car. My father was standing over the camp stove, a cup of coffee in his hand.

"Everyone's in the same fix we are, Margaret. They're just trying to keep their animals alive." He reached out an arm to hug me while continuing to talk. Like Milt, he explained, most of the men had unyoked their oxen and hurried them ahead to the spring.

"Did you see Charlie?" I asked. "Is he still helping out Uncle Jake?"

Pa nodded. "Jake Donner wasn't doing too well to begin with. This desert has really knocked it out of him. He'll need a long rest when we get to the spring, I'm afraid."

Mama tapped me on the shoulder and handed me the canteen she'd been drinking from. Several other canteens hung from Glaucus's saddle.

I took a long gulp. "When will Milt be back?" I asked, thinking about Billy.

"I passed him driving our animals to the spring on my way back last night," Pa answered. "He should have them back any time now."

We stayed outside until the sun became unbearable, then sweltered in the wagon. No one felt like talking, or even reading or playing games, so we just dozed and waited. But by late afternoon, Milt hadn't returned.

"I don't like this, James," Mama finally said. "I don't like this one bit."

"Where *is* he?" Pa asked each hour, ever more agitated. We knew he didn't expect us to answer, but Patty and I shrugged our shoulders miserably each time he asked. Mama repeatedly looked out the palace car door, straining to see signs of Milt and our animals through the heat waves.

The sun was beginning to set behind Pilot Peak when she turned to Pa, arms spread in anger. "Your wife and children can't wait here any longer, James. What are you going to do?"

Pa stared at her a moment, then abruptly climbed out of the wagon and began to saddle Glaucus. "It's another ten miles to the spring. We'll have to walk. Gather up whatever you think we can carry. Milt and I will bring the wagons in later."

We reacted swiftly. I lifted Tommy onto Glaucus's back. We gathered our coats and canteens and began following Pa through the crunchy salt. Patty carried little Cash. I led Glaucus by the reins. Late at night, when the winds started up, Tommy cried from the numbing cold.

FIFTEEN

SEPTEMBER 1846. BILLY.

A week later I stood in the shadow of Pilot Peak, stroking Billy's neck as Pa prepared to bury two of our wagons. We still had our palace car, but it was no longer our home. It was packed full. We now slept in two tents, set up a distance from the other families.

Pa promised Mama he'd come back for the wagons in a year or so. Mama had responded with a single nod, too overwhelmed by our loss to comment. Now she sat in one of the tents with Patty and Tommy, unable to watch.

We'd been camped at the spring for days, searching for lost livestock, bringing in abandoned wagons, and resting the surviving oxen. Scores of cattle and horses had died or disappeared, and most all the dogs died, too. It was a miracle, Aunt Tamsen kept saying, that all party members survived.

What would I tell Mary if I were to write a letter this minute? That Milt never did make it to the spring that night. That soon after Pa passed him in the desert, all our sixteen oxen bolted and disappeared into the dark, delirious from thirst. That Pa and Milt had hunted for them every day since, with no luck. That Charlie had volunteered to go on alone to Sutter's Fort for emergency provisions. That—

"At least yer pony made it through, Puss." It was Ed Breen. He'd walked up behind me and was stroking Billy's withered flanks, a sorrowful expression on his sunburned, freckled face. I was surprised and moved. Mr. Breen had loaned Pa six of his own oxen. Mrs. Breen had made room in one of their wagons for our crop seed. But I hadn't expected kindness from Ed, a rough-and-tumble boy who had no use for girls, including me, unless we were racing our horses.

"Are they tryin' to hide yer things from the Piutes?" he asked. I nodded. The Piutes were poor desert Indians rumored to steal livestock in the night. Pa and the other men suspected they had captured our runaway oxen.

We watched silently as Uncle George and his teamsters joined Pa and Milt at the wagons. After a half hour of digging, they removed the canvas covers. They pushed the wagons onto their sides and into the deep holes, placed furniture and trunks around one, stove and kitchen items around the other, and laid the covers on top. Finally they threw shovelfuls of salt over them until they looked like two oversized graves at the edge of the desert.

My mind's eye could still see what was in them: Grandma's silver, Mama's rocking chair, Pa's books. Back home in Springfield, I'd watched Pa go through them one by one, deciding which ones to take. I'd helped Mama pack the landscapes painted by Grandpa Keyes, who died soon after I was born.

The Great Salt Desert had reduced us—the wealthiest family in the party—to the neediest.

Ed left to help his family get ready to leave. I had just begun to bridle Billy when I heard Mama call out my name. Something in her tone put me on guard. When I turned she was walking toward me.

"I want to talk to you," she said.

Mama placed a hand on Billy's flank and took a deep breath. Her expression was so pained that my body stiffened in alarm. "Once we leave this little spring it will be miles more of the same dry basin," she said. "Billy won't get any stronger out there."

I searched her face, confused. "But don't we have to leave now?"

"Yes, we do. But Billy is better off here."

"But who will—you mean—leave Billy behind?" The thought hit me so hard that I took a step back.

"Keep your voice down, dear." Mama glanced over her shoulder at the tent where Patty and Tommy were resting. "Everyone's upset enough as it is."

Panic rose, choking me. "But Mama, he'll die here by himself!"

"There are Indians all over this basin, Puss. Certainly one will find Billy and give him a good home."

She couldn't mean it. But she did. A dizzying surge of anger shot through me.

"Mama, I'm not giving my pony to a Piute."

Billy must have known we were talking about him. He turned his head to nuzzle my chest.

"He won't get stronger out there," Mama repeated. Her expression was unchanged, and her reasoned tone enraged me. "Does Pa know about this?" I demanded, my voice rising again. I would run to him and cry or beg or do whatever it would take to overrule Mama and keep Billy.

Mama glanced beyond me to the desert, where Pa and the other men were finishing up, then returned her attention to me. "Your father feels terrible about it," she said. "But he loves Billy as much as you do, so he wants to do what's best for him."

Her words struck like blows. It took a moment to absorb them before I cried out, "This is *his* idea? But he *promised*! He promised I could ride Billy all the way to California!"

Mama dropped her hand from Billy's flank. "Billy's condition is not your father's fault, Virginia."

It was the wrong thing to say. Something burst inside me, and the thoughts I'd pushed aside for so long tumbled out.

"Yes, it *is!*"

Of course Billy's condition was my father's fault. All of it— the blind faith in Lansford Hastings, the ignored warnings, the cutoff, the Wasatch and the Salt Desert—all of it was his fault, and Mama knew it as well as I did. Everyone in the Donner Party knew it.

"Don't say that about your father," Mama said. "He's done his best for—"

I burst into furious tears. Mama reached out for me, but I turned away and buried my face in Billy's neck.

"I expect more from you, Virginia. We've all had to sacrifice..." Mama's words trailed off, and her thought went unfinished.

I don't know how long I cried. Eventually Tommy's voice broke through. He was calling my name. I looked up to see his face through the partially opened tent flap. His bottom lip was trembling. Patty's hand closed around his shoulder and drew him back in.

I took several long, shaky breaths as I wiped my eyes and nose. "I'm all right, Tommy," I called out.

Mama hadn't left. She was watching me, knotting the sash of her apron as though grief-stricken, and a slow realization made my cheeks burn with shame.

Of course Mama was grief-stricken. Her own mother was dead. Her children were suffering. Nearly all she owned was being buried in the desert. My outburst had just made matters worse.

What had Charlie called me after we crossed the Kansas River? A brave sort of girl. Was this one of those challenges he mentioned, the ones that called for being brave? If so, it was too big a challenge for me.

But I would try.

"I'm sorry, Mama." I said it loud so Patty and Tommy could hear, even though my voice shook. "You're right. Billy will be better off here with an Indian family."

SIXTEEN

SEPTEMBER 1846. THE HILL.

I walked for hours at a time now, one dusty boot in front of the other, through a continuous stretch of arid land. Charlie had once told me the land between the Wasatch Mountains and the Sierra Nevada Mountains was called the Great Basin. Rivers and streams, he'd explained, were forced to end here because the Sierras blocked them from reaching an ocean. Drained hollows, low ranges, and dry valleys stretched ahead for hundreds of miles.

The Great Basin. I could think of no better name for the rising and falling rows of treeless hills and sparse flatlands. In Springfield, fall was the prettiest season of the year, but here there was nothing to rest my eyes on but clumps of yellowing sagebrush.

We'd finally joined the California Trail at the south fork of a shallow river called the Humboldt, but the Hastings Cutoff had cost us the whole month of August and most of September. Those who'd chosen the California Trail when we broke from them at Little Sandy were weeks ahead of us. In fact, *all* of those traveling to California this summer were ahead of us.

We, the Donner Party, were this year's last pioneers on the California Trail.

Grass here was so sparse the party had split into two groups to provide enough food for our remaining livestock. The Donner families, including Leanna, were now traveling three or four days ahead. That way, after the first group's oxen grazed on the trail, there would be a few days' new growth for the second group's oxen.

My family had lost two wagons, all our furniture, and all our livestock save one milk cow. We were rationing food to two meals a day. I could feel the result by the looseness of my dress. I could see the result in Tommy's face. His baby fat was melting away, exposing sharp cheekbones.

All these troubles, yet my mind kept returning to Billy. A week earlier, his questioning brown eyes had followed our wagon train as it pulled away from Pilot Peak. He stood still as a statue, not bending to eat or drink, as though waiting for me to realize I'd forgotten him and come back.

In the days that followed, Pa tried to convince me we'd saved Billy's life by leaving him behind. Deep down, I knew he was probably right. But that didn't mean my anger had evaporated. After my outburst at Pilot Peak, it seemed impossible to stuff my resentment back to wherever it had been brewing.

Yet my heart ached and my temper flared whenever I overheard others, like Mr. Keseberg or Mr. Graves, blaming Pa in some way for our troubles. The conflicting emotions confused me greatly. If only Charlie were here to talk to!

I kept wondering: Did Pa have any regrets about his mistakes at all? He must, yet he didn't show it. He rode ahead each morning, alone now, to hunt small game or to find our next camp spot. He continued to give opinions on our progress each night at campfire. And his hopes for our life in California seemed unflagging as ever.

One morning after breakfast, Pa went hunting on his own, leaving Milt to drive our palace car up a sandy hill.

The men moved the wagons one by one, triple-yoking teams of oxen for the pull, until only one of Mr. Graves's wagons and our palace car were left. Milt and Mama waited their turn at the bottom while John Snyder started up with the Graveses' wagon.

I was watching Patty and Tommy wade in the Humboldt River when I first heard John's piercing cries. Alarmed, I ran across the sandy soil to where Milt and Mama stood. The Graveses' oxen had come to a complete stop halfway up the hill. John was running back and forth in front of them, cursing and cracking his whip over their heads. The oxen were lowing in fear.

Mama shook her head, bewildered. "Has John Snyder lost his mind?"

Milt creased his brow. "Johnny has a temper, but this isn't like him." He called up the hill. "Watch your language, boy. There's young ones down here."

John stopped cursing, but the veins pulsed in his neck as he glared down the hill at Milt. Then he bared his teeth and turned, striking one of Mr. Graves's oxen with the butt end of his whip.

"John, stop that!" a woman's voice cried out.

My eyes moved farther up the hill. Mary Graves was standing at the top. Milt saw her, too. Her call spurred him into action.

"Johnny's not getting anywhere," he told us. "I'm taking our wagon up alongside to help him."

Mama nodded in agreement, but I suspected Milt's real intent. This was his chance to save the day and impress the young woman he admired at campfire each night.

Pa rode into camp just as Milt was drawing the palace car uphill alongside the Graveses' oxen. Almost immediately, our wagon's lines got entangled with John's. John cursed again, this time at Milt. And then he turned his whip on our oxen.

"Those oxen belong to the Breens," Mama gasped.

"Stop—*stop!*" Pa slid off Glaucus and clambered uphill. But John continued to strike while Milt, yelling for him to stop, tried to untangle the lines. Pa reached John and grabbed for the whip.

"Control yourself!" he shouted. "We need these animals."

"I don't see *you* trying to get them up the hill, Mr. Reed," John shot back. "I don't see you doing anything around here, except put on airs."

Pa must have been stunned by John's insolence. He froze just long enough for the teamster to raise the butt end of the whip and strike hard. Pa fell, and I heard a scream—my own—as Mama hurried uphill toward the bedlam. Milt controlled the terrified oxen while Pa struggled to stand.

Just then Patty caught up to me and clutched my arm.

Pa staggered for balance, his hat on the ground. Blood gushed from his forehead, and he wiped his face with his sleeve. As John raised his whip to strike again, Mama lunged at him from the side and tried to grab it away. In a paralyzing slow-motion moment, John brought the whip down on Mama, and she collapsed. Patty and I both screamed.

By now a crowd had gathered at the top of the hill, yelling for John to stop. Pa took a swing at him. The two men struggled a few seconds more. Then John Snyder dropped to his knees.

The crowd went silent. It took me a long moment to realize Pa's knife was stuck in John's collarbone. John touched the handle, his anger replaced by confusion.

"John." Pa, still staggering, tried to pull the teamster to a standing position. But John's body was going limp. "Oh, no. John. I didn't mean—"

John fell forward. Pa collapsed next to him.

I brushed Patty's hand from my arm and stumbled uphill. By the time I got to my parents, Mama was on her knees, cradling Pa's head. His eyes were closed, and blood was spreading across her lap.

Party members swarmed the scene. In the confusion that followed, Mr. Graves and Mr. Keseberg rolled John on his back and knelt beside him. Milt pulled Pa to his feet and began walking him down the hill. I followed, supporting Mama under one arm.

"Dis isn't over by a long shot, Reed."

I turned to see Mr. Keseberg gripping John's ankles as Mr. Graves slid his hands under the teamster's arms. John's head lolled back lifelessly as the two men lifted him from the ground.

Mr. Keseberg's ice-blue eyes found mine. "You Reeds have gone too far dis time," he said. His voice was strangely calm, and I shuddered.

What did he mean?

The next hour passed in a blur. Milt sat Pa against a rock where we'd been camping, then went back for the palace car. Mama hovered over Pa, dazed and unable to act. She seemed unaware of Patty's tears or Tommy's frightened whimpers.

Bile rose in my throat when I knelt beside him. A three-inch piece of flesh hung from the bloody wound like an open door, exposing part of his skull. I pulled off my sunbonnet and pressed it against his scalp, fighting back nausea as the yellow fabric turned a dark red.

When I thought to glance up the hill, I saw that the rest of the party, including the Graveses' wagon, had disappeared.

Why wasn't anyone helping us? Even the Breens were on the other side of the hill.

Milt brought the palace car back to camp. "That wound needs to be cleaned and stitched," he said.

Pa turned his face toward mine. "Virginia," he said faintly.

I'd been queasy enough while holding my bonnet against Pa's wound. The bitter-tasting bile rose again. How could I possibly stitch it up?

Milt repitched the tent and herded Mama and the children inside. Pa and I climbed into the cramped palace car. He sank onto a pile of clothing while I pulled Mama's sewing box out from under one of the platforms. Thank goodness one of her needles was already threaded. My hands were shaking so, I couldn't possibly have aimed a piece of thread through its eye.

Milt handed up a cup of river water and disappeared. I untied Pa's scarf, dipped it into the cup, and pursed my lips as I gingerly washed and dried the ragged wound. Pa's silence frightened me.

"Does this hurt?" I asked as I pushed the flap closed and dabbed around its edges.

"Don't worry about hurting me, Puss. Just do what you have to."

Stitch by uneven stitch, my trembling fingers poked the needle through the loose flesh and attached it to the skin near his hairline.

"Why was John so angry?" Pa asked, wincing as I worked. His voice sounded young, bewildered. "I didn't mean to hurt him. I was trying to fend him off. He was out of control."

"Hush, Pa. You need to be still while I do this."

If only the Donners hadn't gone on ahead of us, I thought. And Charlie. Why did *he* have to be the one to go to Sutter's

Fort for supplies? Without our friends, we were a family alone, at the mercy of these other families.

"He hit your mother with his whip. Did you see?"

My eyes stung and I blinked to clear them. "It wasn't your fault." I wrapped and rewrapped a wide strip of cloth around his forehead.

Milt leaned through the side door. "I unhitched the oxen. Can I help in here?"

"We have a couple of spare wagon planks left," Pa answered without turning. "Give them to Mr. Graves for Johnny's coffin."

"All right, Mr. Reed." Milt met my eyes and shook his head before he withdrew.

Somehow I managed to stitch up the three-sided wound. But as soon as I finished, I burst into tears. Pa held me for a moment. He smelled of blood and dirt.

"You're a brave girl, Puss."

"No, I'm not. Can we go home now? I want to go home."

He gave my shoulder an awkward pat. "I need to see your mother," he said, then left the wagon and headed for the tent. My fingers were still trembling as I picked up the bonnet Grandma made, now dripping in blood, and carried it to the river. I knelt on the sand and plunged it in, scrubbing the folds of the cloth together. The reddening water turned a sickening pink as it billowed into the current, and this time I let the nausea overwhelm me. I retched, over and over again, into the flowing waters.

SEVENTEEN

SEPTEMBER 1846. BANISHED.

The Graves family didn't want planks for John's coffin. They wanted justice.

Two hours later, while my family sat stunned and silent in our tent, Mr. Graves, Mr. Keseberg, and Mr. Breen walked down the hill to our camp and called out for Pa. All of us, including Patty and Tommy, walked out with him.

I could see by Mr. Graves's blotchy skin that he'd been crying. He drew himself up with a long breath. "We held a meeting to decide what to do about John's murder. A price has to be paid for taking the life of that fine young man."

No one spoke for the few moments it took Mr. Graves's words to sink in. Then I remembered: there were no laws to follow on the frontier.

Pa said evenly, "Surely you know I didn't mean to kill John Snyder."

"Ve saw what happened, Reed," Mr. Keseberg said. I detected a sneer beneath his mustache. "It vas cold-blooded murder. Ve should lynch you for it, but Breen here has persuaded us to let you go on foot."

Mr. Breen drew back. "I didn't say *on foot*," he protested, his brogue pronounced.

Pa squared his shoulders. "You may as well lynch me, Keseberg," he said. "Because I'll not be run off by the likes of you."

"Oh! Don't say that, Pa!" The words escaped me before I could think.

"Dat suits me fine, Reed," Mr. Keseberg shot back, his face reddening. "I've already made a gallows from the tongue of my vagon." His sneer stretched into a smile.

My heart was pounding so hard I was sure it would explode through my chest.

"You should be ashamed, Mr. Keseberg," someone said. I turned. The German's rough words must have jolted my mother from her stupor. She was glaring at him boldly. "This isn't about John Snyder. You've always had it in for my husband." Then she turned to Mr. Graves. "And *you* wouldn't be trying to take over the party this way if George Donner were here."

I caught my breath. I'd never heard Mama speak to a man, not even Pa, the way she was speaking to these two. Mr. Graves's face turned crimson. He looked down at his boots.

Mr. Breen took a step forward, his face so white that his freckles stood out like measles. "James," he pleaded. "I will watch o'er Margaret and the children. The way folks are feelin' right now, you're puttin' yer whole family at risk by stayin'."

"You valk out of here on foot, now," Mr. Keseberg added. "No horse. No rifle. No food."

"I won't go," Pa repeated. But he didn't sound so sure this time.

Tommy suddenly let out a wail. All heads turned toward him, and Patty anxiously tried to shush him.

Mama turned back to Mr. Graves. "John struck me with his whip," she said. "James defended me like any decent husband would."

"That's not the way I saw it," Mr. Graves answered, his voice breaking. He paused for a moment, composing himself. "I got no problem with you, Margaret. You and your children and hired man can travel on with us. But James here has to go."

Then he leveled his gaze back at Pa. "You *should* hang for what you did, Reed. I'll let you take that fancy horse of yours, but no rifle. If you die out there by starvation or by Indians, there's no blood on my hands. It's God's will."

Pa had an hour to leave. Mr. Breen disappeared up the hill after taking Pa aside a few minutes, but Mr. Graves and Mr. Keseberg stood at a distance, side by side, arms crossed, watching. I was numb with disbelief: These two were actually going to make sure my father rode away with nothing but the clothes on his back. I so wanted to cross my arms and glare back at them, but my fear for Pa outweighed my outrage. At this point, they might make him pay for anything his family did.

"Puss." Mama's voice pierced through my seething fog. "I need you. Now."

I followed Mama into the wagon and helped her gather anything Pa could fit into his saddlebag: bandages, scissors, a wool cap.

"They think they're giving him a death sentence," Mama snapped as she searched through the pile of clothing. "We'll see about that." She pulled out a pair of knit gloves. "Puss, get his other neck scarf. Yes, the black one. Stuff that in the bag, too."

By the time I left the tent, Milt had had already resaddled Glaucus. I handed the saddlebag over and looked around for Pa. He was crouched nearby with Patty and Tommy, consoling them with promises of a prompt reunion at Sutter's Fort.

As scared as I was about Pa's banishment, I was more scared at the possibility of a hanging. What if Mr. Graves changed his mind before Pa left? Mr. Keseberg had said the gallows was already in place.

Mama must have feared the same thing. She hurried Pa along as he gave a final hug to us children. Yet once he mounted Glaucus, she clung to the reins, unable to let go.

I held hands with Patty and Tommy to keep them back while my parents said good-bye.

"It will take only a few days to catch up with the Donners," Pa assured Mama, his face dreadfully pale. "They'll give me whatever I need to get to Sutter's Fort."

A lump formed in my throat when he reached into his shirt pocket and handed her the Master Mason medal he was so proud of. "Hold onto this for me," he said, closing his hand over hers.

Then, pointedly ignoring the two men standing nearby, Pa gave Glaucus a command and galloped off.

I wanted to cry out, *Wait Pa. I didn't finish saying good-bye. Look back at me.* But Patty and Tommy both started crying, so I knelt to comfort them.

"We'll see Pa again before we know it," I heard myself say.

Hours later, Mama shook me awake and motioned for me to follow her out of the tent. Milt was waiting in the light of a half moon, his horse saddled. He was holding Pa's rifle.

"There's dried beef and biscuits in here," Mama said, handing me a cloth-wrapped package. "Ammunition, too."

I looked at her questioningly.

"I won't let them send your father into the wilderness without food or protection. I want you and Milt to get these to him."

Standing up to Mr. Keseberg. And now this. I'd never seen this side of my mother. Perhaps, with Pa around to take care of things, she'd had no need to reveal it. I gave her an impulsive hug.

Milt mounted his horse and pulled me up behind him. I wrapped my arms firmly around his waist, and for a few aching seconds a memory washed over me: I was five years old again, riding Glaucus behind Pa.

We followed the curve of the Humboldt through a valley too narrow for wagons. A mile or so from camp, when he was sure we couldn't be seen from the hill, Milt steered his horse back to the trail.

It must have been past midnight when we saw the glow from Pa's campfire. He was staring into the flames, his bandage bloodstained, his face etched with sadness. Nothing that had happened—Grandma's death, losing the wagons in the desert, or watching Billy disappear behind me—tore at me like seeing my father so grief stricken.

I slid from Milt's horse and started running. "I'm coming with you! I'm going to take care of you!"

Pa rose and I slammed into his arms. He rocked me side to side for a moment, then held me out by the shoulders. "No, Puss, you're as faithful a daughter as I could ask for, but it's your mother who needs you now."

I dissolved into tears, and Pa hugged me again while Milt set down the food and rifle. Then Pa sat me down by the fire.

"Wait here."

He and Milt walked several feet away, whispering urgently while I watched the flames and wiped my eyes.

A faithful daughter? I'd deceived Pa for months with my rosary necklace and secret prayers. I'd blamed him for his mistakes and for having to leave Billy at the spring. And all the while, Pa was doing the best he knew how.

I hadn't been a faithful daughter.

"Puss," he called out after a few minutes. "You took an awful risk by bringing me this rifle." He walked to the campfire and crouched beside me. "You can't tell anyone you did this. I don't want more trouble for you or your mother."

He reached for my hand and squeezed it. "I killed a man today, Puss. A good man. It's best I go on."

"Mr. Reed, don't you talk like that," Milt said, sitting beside us. "It was self-defense and they all know it. Those men been jealous of you from the start." He lifted his chin defiantly. "They was just looking for an excuse to kick you out."

I expected such loyalty from Milt. But I saw things more clearly now. Perhaps some of the men had once been jealous, but for a long time they'd simply been angry. Too many willful decisions. Too many serious mistakes. John Snyder's death was the last straw.

"I think I can turn this whole thing around, Milt," Pa said. "We don't know when Charlie will get back with provisions. In any case, there's only so much he can carry. I'll go on to Sutter's Fort and get more food for all of us."

I stared at Pa, incredulous. He was transforming his banishment into a relief mission before my eyes. The color returned to his face as he and Milt continued talking.

For better or for worse, Pa was already on to his next plan.

EIGHTEEN

SEPTEMBER 1846. ALONE.

"Hold your head high, Virginia," Mama said as we started up the hill early the next morning. She lifted her chin as she took Tommy's hand.

I was sluggish with grief and fatigue, but I straightened my spine and reached out for Patty. A grim-faced Milt, hat pulled over his eyes, followed alongside the oxen as they pulled the palace car.

Patty had run out of tears. She looked as sorrowful as I felt. Her hand was dry and weightless in mine, a withered leaf. I squeezed it, hoping to get a squeeze back, just to assure myself my little sister was still there. But there was no response.

The sun rose behind us, turning the sky a clear, pale blue, but the early morning cold stung my face. Gritty sand slid beneath my boots as we made our way up the hill. My stomach clenched painfully when we passed the location of yesterday's fight.

Mama's voice dropped to a whisper when we reached the top. "Don't talk to anyone except the Breens."

The Breens, Kesebergs, and other families were breaking camp and preparing to chain up. Nearby, the large Graves family was clustered around John Snyder's final resting place. Gold desert flowers were strewn over the freshly turned mound, marked by a hastily fashioned wooden cross.

The sight of John's grave jolted me. I'd been so caught up with Pa's banishment that I'd barely considered the death of the handsome teamster. Now I remembered him dropping to his knees, his hands moving up to Pa's knife, his anger turning to bewilderment. I remembered Pa, half-blind from his own blood, trying to pull John to a standing position, as though that could reverse what he'd done.

A new wave of grief pulsed through me. John Snyder was dead. It seemed impossible. Why, only two nights ago at camp-fire, I'd clapped along with the others while he and Mary Graves tried out a new dance called the polka. Now as I looked from the cross to Mary's tear-stained face, I realized John Snyder would never get to California. He would never marry his sweetheart.

But why had he attacked my parents? It was unexplainable. I saw Mama's back stiffen as we joined the others, and my grief gave way to anger as I remembered how John had struck her to the ground. Because of John Snyder, my father was alone on the frontier, and my family was at the mercy of those who had banished him.

Pa, I realized now, was right to send me back last night. I couldn't leave Mama and the children alone with only Milt to help. Suddenly, with Pa gone, I was the other grownup in the family.

We walked near the end of the wagon train, close behind the Breens and in front of the remaining cattle, as the party plodded along the rutted trail. I'd braced myself for angry words from others, or at least some unkind looks, but no one paid us any mind. Few spoke, and families kept to themselves. Most everyone was walking, trying to save the strength of the remaining oxen by keeping wagons light as possible. Still, our progress was painfully slow under the cloudless sky, as though the party was dragging a great weight of sadness.

That day, whether walking silently beside our wagon, sharing a sober meal with the children, or saying silent prayers in my heart, the grim reality of Pa's banishment continued to wash over me afresh. That night, I trembled in my bed, thinking of Pa sleeping alone in the wilderness. Yet, I reminded myself, what *could* have happened was even worse. Mr. Keseberg had pushed Mr. Graves for a lynching. I shuddered in half sleep, remembering the German's description of his wagon tongue angled against the sky, and how his eagerness to use it as a gallows had distorted his smile. I sat up in confusion, thinking for a moment that Pa had been hanged.

The next day I kept my eyes on the sage-covered ground, searching for signs that Pa was safely ahead of us. At dusk, as the party circled the remaining wagons, Mama found a cold campfire off-trail near the river and called the family over. Feathers and shell casings were scattered about.

Milt joined us. He crouched down to inspect the site, stirring the ashes with a stick. "He's a half day ahead, Mrs. Reed," he said, squinting up at us. "He should catch up with the Donners in another day or two." He gestured at the feathers as he stood. "And he's finding food."

"See that, Tommy?" Patty said, clapping her hands. "Pa shot and ate a bird."

Tommy smiled and nodded, but Mama didn't seem comforted. "Two more days? I hope it doesn't take that long, Milt."

I stared out at the emptiness ahead. Nothing but more sage and scatterings of low hills. Was Pa lonely out there? Was he afraid?

Later, as I scrubbed dishes upriver, I saw Mr. Graves and Mr. Keseberg standing over Pa's campfire. I stopped moving until they left, my hands growing cold in the icy water. They would see the spent casings! Why hadn't we removed them?

But neither man asked Mama how Pa had got hold of his rifle. In fact, they both seemed to have lost interest in Pa. They had new concerns.

There was a foreboding chill in the air, and not only at night. It was hanging on well through midmorning—a warning, Mr. Graves claimed, of early winter.

And there was still no sign of Charlie.

That night Mr. Graves called a meeting for everyone, even the women and children. As my family sat at a distance from the others, he proposed we all combine whatever food we had left and start rationing as a group.

"We're running out," he declared, lacing his fingers together and leaning toward the campfire. "Charles Stanton should have been back from Sutter's Fort with provisions by now. How long can it take one man on horseback, anyway?"

Mr. Keseberg called out, "Vo's to say he ever planned to come back?"

Mama and I exchanged an indignant expression. Of course Charlie planned to come back.

"I can't be sharin' my food," Mr. Breen objected. "I have seven children to feed."

"I have a large family, too." Mr. Graves answered, his voice thickening. "There are twelve of us altogether."

"You've been careless with your food supply, Graves. *My* family has cut down to one meal a day," Mr. Keseberg said.

"They have *not*," Patty said under her breath. "He's lying, Mama."

Mama patted her hand. "Hush, Patty."

I didn't want Patty and Tommy to witness more anger building among the men. "Let's go," I said, standing.

I gathered the children, but Mama remained sitting and listening.

Mr. Graves ran a hand through his graying hair. "Share or not, none of us is going to make it to California unless we get food from Sutter's Fort, and soon."

"Pa's bringing back food for us," I heard myself say. All faces turned toward me. I stared back, voiceless, startled by my own outburst.

Mama stood and gave my arm a reassuring squeeze. She lifted her chin. "That's right. Despite his unfair treatment, my husband intends to return from Sutter's Fort with provisions for everyone."

Mr. Graves scowled in the firelight before answering. "That could take weeks, Margaret. We don't *have* weeks. No, if anyone gets food to us in time, it'll be Stanton." With that he stood up and strode away from the campfire, muttering and shaking his head.

In time? In time for what? And what did Mr. Graves mean by our running out of food? *Completely?* How could the grownups let that happen? With no food, we'd be stuck in this basin—unable to go on to California, unable to go back home. And then what would we eat?

I wasn't the only one shaken by Mr. Graves's words. Everyone was stunned silent. Family by family, they rose and returned to their wagons.

I didn't sleep at all that night. Snuggling next to Tommy's warmth, I wondered how many of the grownups already regretted banishing Pa. He'd been blamed for our troubles, but without his leadership the Donner Party was unraveling into a loose collection of frightened families, all out for themselves.

"I'm scared, Pa," I whispered into the dark. "Get back here soon."

Two days later the trail led us into a narrow canyon bordered by low cliffs. Mr. Graves, who was riding ahead, found a note tucked in the shallow branches of a sage bush.

"It's from James Reed," he said, extending the scrap of paper to Mama. "You should read it first, Margaret."

Mama stared at Mr. Graves stonily as she unfolded the small piece of paper. But her face paled when she scanned the words. She handed it to Mr. Breen.

By now most party members had gathered around, waiting expectantly. "Piutes killing Donner oxen," Mr. Breen read aloud. His brow creased and he looked up. "It says we should stay close together."

The Irishman shook his head as he handed the note back to Mama. "We were shortsighted to banish James," he said. "With Indians trying to kill our cattle, we can't afford to lose a single man. And now we've lost two."

"Yes, two. Because James Reed *murdered* da other one," Mr. Keseberg shot back angrily, as though we Reeds weren't standing right there, listening.

Patty tugged at Mama's skirt. "What about Pa? Will he be all right?"

Her question echoed my thoughts. What if the Piutes tried to steal Glaucus? Pa had his rifle, but was that really enough to protect one man traveling alone?

Mama didn't answer. She was scanning the hills that surrounded us.

I placed my hand on Patty's shoulder. "Pa can take care of himself. We've seen the campfire and feathers. He'll catch up with the Donners soon, anyway."

But an hour later we came upon four oxen dead near the trail. Arrows rose from their carcasses like signposts. Chunks of their flesh were cut away. I turned my head in disgust.

Mr. Breen swore aloud. "The hell with splittin' up for grazin' purposes. We'd better catch up with the Donners and travel as one group again."

That night the men set up double shifts to guard our cattle.

At first light I awoke to rifle shots, men yelling in confusion, and cattle lowing in pain. Then quiet. My heart pounded through my chest, but the terrifying sounds had lasted such a short time I hoped that maybe I'd dreamed them. Just the same, I crawled from the tent and ran until I was outside the wagon circle.

My stomach slowly turned and sank. Shotgun smoke hung in the air, its acrid smell burning my nostrils. Four or five men moved among dead and wounded animals like morning shadows. Eventually, I recognized Milt's silhouette. He was waving his arms and yelling something in my direction. That's when I realized Mama was standing beside me.

"They showered arrows on us for sport, Mrs. Reed." Even in the smoky dawn I could see how his face was contorted with rage. He pointed to a nearby hill. "We could hear them laughing. *Laughing!*"

The sob in his voice shook me so much that I struggled to swallow my own sob.

"How many?" Mama called out. But Milt had turned away.

More than a dozen cattle died that morning—some killed outright, others wounded and later butchered by their owners. The oxen we'd borrowed from the Breens were among them.

All that morning Mama sat on the palace car steps, stunned. She shook her head when I offered her coffee. I cooked corn-meal mush for Patty and Tommy, gave little Cash a tough, dry strip of meat, and answered the children's questions best I could. Then I sat beside Mama, my arm around her shoulders. The men stood a distance away, talking. Eventually Mr. Breen broke from the group and walked toward us, his eyes on the ground. Mama looked up, and I felt her shoulders stiffen beneath my arm.

"You'll have to leave yer wagon behind, Margaret. We've no more oxen to lend you." The Irishman nodded toward his wagons. "We can carry some of yer things."

"Oh, no, Mr. Breen," I protested. "Please."

Mama pressed her fingers against her forehead and slowly shook her head. "This wagon holds the last of all we own, Patrick."

"I know. I know." His voice came out strangled and high-pitched.

Mr. Graves and his wife, a sallow, pinch-faced woman, approached us. Mr. Graves cleared his throat.

"Margaret, I know how you feel about me." His jowls jiggled as he spoke. "We have to put that aside for now. We can carry a few of your things in one of my wagons. We'll make room somehow."

"This isn't a time for false pride, Margaret," Mrs. Graves added. I sent the woman a sharp look. Had I heard a tinge of smugness in her voice? "It's a sacrifice for us," she continued, "but as good Christians, we're willing."

Mama dropped her hands to her lap, and for a moment I feared she might refuse their offer. But without looking up, she rose and said, "Well, we'd better sort through our belongings, then. We have to get out of here."

Mrs. Graves's eyes flared. She started to say something more, but Mr. Graves shushed her.

The children and I followed Mama into the palace car and numbly began to search through canvas bags for the warmest of what was left of our clothing.

"Mama, is there room for Elsa?" Patty asked, holding up the one porcelain doll she'd saved when Pa buried our belongings. Mama looked over her shoulder and shook her head, then resumed sorting through clothes.

"This one, then?" Patty held up the tiny wooden doll Hardcoop had carved for her. "She's so little."

Mama didn't even turn to look. "No, Patty." Her tone was sharp. "There's no *room.*" Patty flinched.

Mama wasn't making sense, but this was no time for an argument. I shook my head at Patty, hoping she wouldn't start crying—Mama might not be able to bear it.

But Patty didn't cry. Instead, she dragged the blue-flowered quilt from Grandma's old bed down the steps and laid it on the sandy soil within the wagon circle. She called Tommy over, and together they watched Mr. Graves and Mr. Breen pack our family's few salvaged items into their own wagons.

One by one, I pulled each piece of clothing from the last bag. My shell jewelry case rolled out of a long-unused petticoat and its lid fell open, scattering the contents. I gasped. With a quick glance at Mama's back, I grabbed my rosary necklace, slipped it over my head and tucked it under my collar.

The Kesebergs also had to leave a wagon behind. "You go on ahead of us," Mr. Keseberg shouted out as the rest of us prepared to leave. He and old Hardcoop were unloading canvas bags. "I have more work to do here. Ve'll catch up."

Milt lifted Tommy onto his horse's wide back and led him by the reins. The rest of my family left camp on foot, leaving the palace car and the dreams it stood for behind.

This time I didn't look back.

Nineteen

September 1846. Hardcoop.

The sun was nearly overhead and we were nooning near the bank of the Humboldt River when one of Uncle George's teamsters rode into camp. "We've been waiting for you since yesterday," he said as he dismounted. "We're camped some hours up the trail."

There were no real trees here, just a few tall manzanita bushes. Mama and I were sitting beneath them, trying to stay cool in the disappearing shade. She'd oddly decided I should take up crochet on the trail and had just demonstrated a complex stitch for me.

"Now you," she said.

"I already know that one, Mama. Grandma taught me *ages* ago."

"Mrs. Reed." The teamster caught Mama's eye. "Mr. Reed caught up with us yesterday. He borrowed one of the men and went on to Sutter's Fort. He wanted you to know he's all right."

A little cry escaped Mama, and she impulsively kissed me on the cheek. "Well," she said, recovering herself, "I knew he'd be fine all along." She called out to Patty and Tommy, who were wading several feet away. "Children, did you hear that?"

I stood and watched as party members gathered around the teamster for more information. "How long do you think it will take Reed to get back here with food?" Mr. Graves asked. My hand tightened around the crochet hook. Even *he*, I thought bitterly, seemed relieved to hear that Pa was alive and well.

Red and gray streaks crossed the western sky when we finally saw the Donners' six wagons silhouetted on the horizon. Closer to camp, when I saw Leanna poke her head from her family wagon I was so happy I broke into a run. A moment later she was running toward me, then hugging me. "Puss!"

Her body felt slight beneath her coat.

Within a few minutes Aunt Tamsen and Aunt Betsy had settled our family around their campfire, and Mama was deep in a hushed conversation with them. Patty and Tommy resumed playing with the little Donner children as if no time had passed.

"Let's talk by ourselves," Leanna said, taking my hand as Mr. Keseberg drove his remaining wagon into camp. "I was so scared for you, especially after your father told us what happened."

We wandered away from the others and settled ourselves on the ground outside the circle. I'd just begun to tell Leanna the details of what happened between Pa and John Snyder when we heard raised voices in the direction of the Keseberg wagon. When Uncle George walked over to investigate, Leanna and I followed.

"Then you have to backtrack and find him," Mr. Breen was saying, his voice tinged with disbelief. His hands were on his hips, and he was leaning toward Mr. Keseberg. "Ye can't leave an old man alone out there."

"What's going on here?" Uncle George asked, looking from one man to another.

"Hardcoop is missing." Mr. Breen glared accusingly at the German.

Missing? I stared out at the vast expanse behind us. The land was beginning to fade into shadow.

"I don't know vat happened to him," Mr. Keseberg sputtered, his face coloring. "Da last time I looked, he vas valking behind my wagon." He turned and began to unstrap his horse's saddle as though the matter was finished.

"We're not abandonin' an old man," Mr. Breen said, his Irish brogue taking hold. "Someone has to go back out there and bring 'im in."

"And then vat?" the German turned, his face redder. "Do any of you have a horse to spare? Do you have vagon space, or extra food? Because I don't."

I looked again at the darkening space behind us. How far back was Mr. Hardcoop? Was he hurt?

Mama and the Donner women had joined the group by now. "We're not going another mile until we find that old man," Aunt Tamsen declared, her sharp eyes boring through Mr. Keseberg. The air was thick with tension. Leanna grabbed my hand.

Mr. Keseberg took a step toward Aunt Tamsen. "Oh really? Vich one of you is going to look for him? Because it's not going to be me."

There was a dismayed silence. Then Uncle George said, "We'll build a bonfire. Hopefully, he'll see it and find his way here by morning. If he doesn't, we'll look for him then."

Aunt Tamsen turned to her husband. "But George—" she protested.

"It's almost dark," Uncle George said, cutting her off. "He's nowhere in sight. There is nothing else we can do."

Mr. Hardcoop's disappearance had filtered down to the children by bedtime.

"You and Milt can find him in the morning, Puss," Patty said as she and Tommy settled under quilts in our tent. "The same way you found Pa."

I thought of Milt's broken-down horse, our *only* horse, now being used to carry Tommy. I didn't know how to answer her.

Mama, tucking Patty in, kissed her on the forehead. "Let's just hope that poor old man shows up on his own. I'm going to pray for him."

"But if he doesn't," Patty insisted, "then Puss and Milt will find him."

Late that night I prayed for Mr. Hardcoop, too. While the others slept beside me, I pulled the rosary necklace from beneath my collar and grasped its crucifix. Despite my whispered words, the small piece of cold metal felt lifeless in my hand. I fell asleep, waiting for a sense of comfort that never came.

The men fed the bonfire all night, but the next morning the old Belgian was nowhere in sight. At nine o'clock Uncle George ordered us to break camp.

I went numb with disbelief when I realized the Donner Party was doing the unthinkable: abandoning one of its members.

"Mama," I whispered as she lifted Tommy onto Milt's horse. "Do you think Mr. Keseberg left Mr. Hardcoop behind on purpose?"

"This wouldn't be happening if your father was here," was all she said. Her eyes shone with angry tears.

Aunt Tamsen and Aunt Betsy joined us, their faces blotched from crying. "God forgive us all," Aunt Betsy said, embracing Mama. "This isn't who we are."

Still, we left.

The grownups were silent as we started out, but the children pestered their parents with questions.

"Did Mr. Hardcoop get back?"

"Aren't we going to look for him?"

"Is that old man going to catch up with us later?"

"What's going to happen to him out there, Puss?" Patty asked as we walked from camp, side by side.

"Well, he can still catch up, or maybe another wagon will pick him up."

My voice trailed off. I was lying like the grownups. There were no other wagons behind us.

I turned over Aunt Betsy's words—*this isn't who we are*. But we've left Mr. Hardcoop behind, I thought. This *is* who we are now.

Patty was quiet for a long while before she said, "If they leave old people who can't keep up, they'll leave little children who can't keep up, too."

I reached out for her hand and squeezed. "No they won't, Patty."

"Promise me."

"Promise what?" The morning air was biting, and I shivered.

"Promise me you'll never leave me behind."

"Patty. What are you saying? Of course I won't."

"Or Tommy either."

"Stop it."

"Promise."

I glanced down at her, upset. Patty's little face was chalk white.

I softened my voice. "I'll never leave you behind, Patty. I promise."

TWENTY

OCTOBER 1846. RELIEF.

The sun cast lengthening shadows as our party followed a branch of the Humboldt River to a marshy lakebed. I sniffed the air and wrinkled my nose.

"It smells like rotten eggs," Tommy whined.

"Hush," Mama said.

Suddenly I had a vision of Pa sitting at the kitchen table last year in Springfield, reading out loud from the *Sangamon Journal*.

"There's a place out west where rivers end in the middle of nowhere," he exclaimed. "Listen to this pioneer's description, Puss. It's in his letter to the editor.

> 'The sink is a flat, marshy area where the Humboldt River fans out, becomes muddy and sluggish, and produces an unpleasant stench before disappearing into the ground completely.' "

He lifted his head and grinned boyishly. "They call it the Humboldt Sink. Doesn't that beat all!"

The unbidden memory filled me with painful longing. What I wouldn't give to be back home, listening to Pa read to the family as he anticipated the adventures ahead.

The memory faded as we drew closer to the foul odor's source. Dying cattails and other plants were decomposing in the hazy waters.

Nearly everyone in the party groaned in protest when Uncle George announced we would camp here for the night. But as dreadful as the sink was, what lay ahead was sure to be worse. Another desert separated us from the next river we would follow—the Truckee.

That evening Uncle George walked from family to family, trying to calm our fears. "It's only forty miles across, and it's not like the Salt Desert," he assured Mama as she and I handed out strips of dried beef to Patty and Tommy. He smiled encouragingly. "We won't have hundred-degree heat to suffer through. And we're traveling lighter now."

"Much lighter," Mama said, turning away.

Uncle George let her remark pass. But I pondered it as I sat by the fire next to Tommy and chewed the tough beef. Yes, we were traveling much lighter because of our lost wagons and belongings. But Mama, I was sure, wasn't talking about *things*.

Grandma. Pa. Charlie. And Billy. I missed them so much I ached all over.

Early the next morning Milt helped us prepare for the crossing by filling canteens and buckets with the smelly water. "I'll be up ahead with the Donner teamsters, Mrs. Reed," he said. "They're going to need help getting the oxen across this desert."

Patty and Tommy joined the smaller Donner children in the wagons. Mama and I walked behind with Leanna and Aunt Tamsen. My stomach tightened as we started across the bleak landscape. What did it matter if this desert wasn't made of salt? We were still going to be walking for days without a river nearby.

The forty-mile stretch of coarse brown sand and sagebrush had been cruel to those who'd gone before us. Our little caravan passed by rotting axles, deserted farm equipment, and abandoned wagons filled with sand drifts.

All except the smallest children walked to keep the wagons light as possible. Occasional gusts blew sand into our eyes and hair, but Uncle George had been right; this desert was not nearly as deadly as the Salt Desert. Our two-day crossing was uneventful. Just the same, deep sand tugged at the sun-bleached wagon wheels and drained the remaining oxen of energy.

Was the Sierra getting *any* closer? I studied the wavy silhouette on the western horizon. Uncle George said the mountain range was only fifty miles away now, but it didn't look any closer than yesterday, or the day before.

The next afternoon we spotted rows of tall red and gold foliage swaying against a background of small hills.

"Trees!" Milt shouted. "Our first trees in months!"

The children cheered as though Milt had just announced there was candy up ahead. Aspen and cottonwood meant the barren plains and deserts of the Great Basin were behind us forever. We had reached the Truckee River, which we would follow into the Sierra Nevada Mountains.

Leanna tugged at my arm. "Let's get wet, Puss!" She broke into a run and I quickly followed. When we got to the banks, we laughed with pleasure. The fast-moving waters broke and fell over rock piles and fallen branches, spraying foam in the air and forming small, still pools near shore.

Leanna and I unlaced our boots, lifted our skirts, and waded into the chilly current. Children rushed in behind us and started splashing. Once the Breen boys joined us, the water fight got serious. We were all happily soaked in a matter of minutes.

The men cut down some of the trees and built a communal bonfire where we shivered ourselves dry.

That evening Uncle George called for a quick meeting. Mama and I joined the small group that gathered near the campfire.

"It's time to talk about rationing the rest of our food," he announced as he sat next to Uncle Jake.

"You're vasting your breath." Mr. Keseberg, standing, folded his arms across his chest. The firelight revealed his belligerent frown. "Ve already had this conversation before ve caught up with you, George. Nobody is going to make me share what's mine without a fight."

"But Lewis," Uncle George urged quietly, "There are some in our party who have lost most everything."

"I'm with Keseberg," Mr. Graves stated matter-of-factly. He and Mrs. Graves sat directly across from us, and his fleshy face looked more florid than usual. "I'm not asking for anything, and I'm not giving anything away."

"But a week ago you were the one that wanted to—" I said, confused by Mr. Graves's change of mind. Mama squeezed my arm.

"But Mama—"

She shook her head.

Mr. Graves and Mr. Keseberg both looked mean again—like when they banished Pa. This time it was Uncle George they were glaring at. No one spoke. There was only the crackling sound of burning wood. I tried to swallow the lump in my throat. Kind, gentle Uncle George was no match for these two.

"Hey, what's that?"

Heads turned in the direction of Ed Breen's voice. He was standing several feet from the campfire, peering west toward the hilly shadows.

"Do you see that?" he asked. He turned his freckled face toward us for a second before looking west again, one hand shielding his eyes from the setting sun.

Every set of eyes followed his gaze. "I don't see anythin', son," Mr. Breen said, squinting.

"I do," Milt said. He pointed his long arm to the base of a hill a half mile or so away. "Something's moving down there."

"Horses," Ed Breen said. "Horses and men."

I studied the silhouettes as they made their way toward us. Four pack mules led by three riders. I squinted. The lead rider was shorter than the other two. He wore a narrow-brimmed hat. He stood up in his saddle and waved.

"It's Charlie," I said.

I barely felt the sandy soil beneath my stocking feet as I ran toward him. Animated voices followed close behind. Charlie was smiling and waving frantically now. But as I got closer, his forehead creased and his smile faded.

"Puss?" he asked. "Is that you?" He slid off Banjo and studied me a moment before setting his face back into a smile. The beginnings of a beard framed his chin. He hugged me lightly and then stepped back. "Looks like I got back none too soon."

"What do you mean?" I asked, but Charlie had already turned to greet Mama. Then the Donners and the Breens surrounded him, slapping him on the back and nearly suffocating him with hearty hugs.

Maybe he didn't hear my question.

"Hey," he laughed. "Who's going to help me unload these supplies? I've got meat, flour, coffee."

Hungry eyes turned toward the four mules and their packs. The argument over food was abruptly forgotten. Now there was dried beef for all. Flour, too. My mouth watered when I realized I'd soon be eating bread again.

Several party members were staring at the two dark-skinned, longhaired riders in shirts and trousers who had arrived with Charlie.

"Their names are Luis and Salvador," he said. "Members of the Miwok tribe."

The young men nodded shyly when they heard their names, and Charlie gave them a reassuring nod. "They work for Captain Sutter. They don't understand much English, but they know the country between here and Sutter's Fort."

The group shifted uncomfortably, and a low murmur ran through the crowd. *Indians.*

"These men are Christians," Charlie explained patiently. "We have Captain Sutter to thank for them. And for this food, too. He'll send more with Mr. Reed's relief party."

Had I heard Charlie right? *Mr. Reed's* relief party!

Mama, who was crouched down whispering to Patty and Tommy, rose a bit. "What was that you said?"

Charlie grinned. "We crossed paths on the trail, Margaret. James was nearly to Sutter's Fort by then. He may already be on his way back to us with more provisions."

Hours later, after most everyone fell asleep well fed, I sat alone by the campfire, thinking.

Charlie had been gone little more than six weeks, yet he hadn't recognized me at first. I fingered the fraying cloth of my blue plaid dress. I knew I'd shrunk inside it. The budding curves I'd noticed on the plains had melted away. I was wearing Pa's heavy jacket to keep warm, and an old bonnet of Aunt Betsy's replaced my bloodstained yellow one. But did I really look that different from the last time he saw me?

Did we all look different?

Surely, walking up to fifteen miles on one meal a day had made all of us, even Mr. Graves, skinnier. But maybe Charlie saw something else. While he was gone, desperation had evolved into arguments among the men, anger among the mothers, and pitiful crying among the littlest children.

The fear that haunted us must have shown up on our faces.

None of this mattered now, I assured myself. Everything was going to be all right. We had food again. Pa was on his way. And only the Sierra stood between us and California.

TWENTY ONE

OCTOBER 1846. ONWARD.

"I don't understand why people are surprised he came back to help us," I said to Mama the next morning as I sat on a flat rock, lacing my battered boots. Mama sat beside me, brushing Patty's hair with firm, hard strokes. Patty winced with each pull, but stayed stoically silent. "People think just because he's single, he has no ties here."

Mama laid the brush down and started braiding. "Charlie's a man of honor, like your father. It would never occur to him to think of himself while we are in need. Remember how he told us about all the years he spent caring for his sick mother? I'm sure that's why he never married."

Charlie was now the party's authority on the Sierra, having crossed it twice now. So after savoring breakfasts of johnny-cakes for the first time in weeks, the party gathered around him. The air was cold; rain clouds were forming. Leanna and I huddled close to the fire, watching our breath turn into little puffs as Charlie stood to describe what lay ahead.

"Truckee Meadows is two days away," he said, turning his narrow-brimmed hat with his fingers. "It's wide and level—and there's enough grass for several days' grazing."

"Surely you're not sayin' we should camp there fer more than a night." Mr. Breen turned his face to the sky. "It's about to rain. That means snow in the mountains. We can't dillydally there."

"There are flurries on the summit at night," Charlie admitted. "But the pass is wide open. Sutter says it won't be blocked for another month."

The men were silent, but Charlie must have sensed their discomfort.

"Boys," he said, "I understand why you're impatient. But listen to me. The oxen have to gain strength. The Sierra is like nothing we've climbed so far. The ascent from Truckee Lake through the pass is brutal—worse than the Wasatch."

Worse than the Wasatch! I scooted closer to the fire's warmth. How could the ascent be worse? Why, the California Trail through the Sierra was well traveled. There should be no hacking of trees or bushes, no pushing of heavy rocks.

Charlie's voice, more forceful now, broke through my thoughts. "The pass through the summit is fifty miles west of Truckee Meadows. But first we'll reach a flat, wooded area called Alder Creek. The lake sits a few miles beyond that—"

And somewhere in between, I thought, we'll meet up with Pa.

"—and from there it's a steep climb to the summit. Once we reach the pass, it's easier going. We'll wind down another hundred miles to the valley floor."

"Nothing you've just described sounds vorse than the Vasatch," Mr. Keseberg said.

Charlie paused before answering. "The climb from the lake to the pass is short, but you'll be pulling wagons up granite cliffs," he said. "It's difficult in the best of conditions, but your wagons are barely holding together. Your oxen are very weak, and so are all of you."

Mr. Keseberg shifted uncomfortably, but said nothing more.

Uncle George pushed himself up and clapped Charlie on the back. "Let's start out, boys," he said. "We can be on our way in less than an hour if we put our minds to it."

Charlie insisted Mama ride one of the mules, and she gratefully accepted. The other two mules packed food and other supplies. Patty and Tommy each rode behind an Indian scout. Patty looked unsure when Milt lifted her and set her firmly behind Salvador. But Tommy, his short arms wrapped around Luis and his sombrero firmly on his head, beamed broadly as he turned to see if the Breen boys were watching. My heart jumped when Charlie said I'd be riding Banjo with him.

As Mr. Breen had predicted, a light rain started falling as we left camp. My family was in the lead: the others followed close behind.

The bonnet Aunt Betsy lent me was soon soaked, and Milt gave me his threadbare wool scarf and stained, wide-brimmed leather hat. I pushed the hat back and pressed my forehead between Charlie's shoulders. I sat that way all day, eyes closed, feeling the swaying motion of his horse as we crossed and re-crossed the river. This was the happiest I'd felt in a long time. Charlie was close as he could be. Pa was on his way with a relief party. Soon we would all be together in California.

Occasionally I lifted my head and glimpsed the Sierra through the rain. It was finally getting closer, its peaks covered by dark clouds. I shivered. Snow must be falling up there.

That night during a break in the rain, I was still up, wrapped in the buffalo robe and wistfully watching the river flow eastward. Earlier Charlie had explained that, unlike other rivers west of the Continental Divide, the Truckee started high in the Sierra and flowed down its eastern slopes.

"Best to join your ma and the other children in the tent," Charlie said as he walked out of the dark toward me. "We have an early start tomorrow. We want to reach the meadows before nightfall."

The other *children*! The word struck my heart with a thud. I'd grown up a lot since Pa's banishment, but Charlie still saw me as the Reeds' oldest child. For a moment I couldn't speak.

He crouched down across from me. "Virginia? Are you all right?"

Yet how could he understand all that had happened while he was gone? I wasn't being fair. I struggled to compose myself.

"Tell me what California's like," I said finally, hoping to make him stay awhile. "Is it beautiful like they say?"

Charlie sat down, crossing his legs. He took out his pipe. "More beautiful. The foothills are golden and filled with wildlife. The valley is flat and green, and stretches all the way to the Pacific Ocean. The people I met are kindhearted and generous."

He lit the pipe and exhaled. "You'll love it there."

I doubt *that*, I thought, watching the river's eastward flow. Eastward, toward Springfield. Toward home.

California could never be beautiful enough to be worth all we'd left behind.

And that's when the words tumbled out. Charlie sat with me another hour, sometimes silent, sometimes offering words of comfort, while I tearfully described the heartbreak of Billy's abandonment, the horror surrounding Pa's banishment, and the shameful desertion of old Hardcoop.

By the time we reached Truckee Meadows, the sky had cleared and the sun was setting over rich grasslands marked with cottonwood groves. The Sierra loomed above us—rocky and forbidding.

Uncle George and Mr. Breen approached Charlie as he helped me off Banjo.

"I think we should press on tomorrow mornin'." Mr. Breen's brogue was stronger than usual again. "As long as the sun's out, the snow will be melting. We can hurry through the pass."

Charlie shook his head. "We won't make it. Look at that mountain. Then look at your oxen."

I followed the men's eyes as they turned from the rugged peaks to the open fields where the gaunt animals grazed.

Uncle George sighed. "He's right, Patrick. They need to get stronger. Besides, I need to work on an axle."

"It's decided then," Charlie said. "We'll camp here to prepare for the climb."

Mr. Breen's worried expression didn't change, but he didn't argue, either. I thought he probably wasn't ready to climb the Sierra any more than I was. I'd been riding horseback behind Charlie the past two days, but my body ached as though I'd been crawling. Others, I noted, looked as tired as I felt. Like me, they were probably relieved that someone else had made the decision for us.

We camped for five days, drying our wet clothes and blankets under sunny skies. The grownups' tempers improved, now that everyone had plenty to eat. We not only had the food that Charlie brought, we had abundant wildlife, too. Some of the men set out with shotguns and came back with rabbits and squirrels for supper.

On the evening before we were to leave, Uncle George sliced his hand while repairing his axle. His arm became blue and swollen during the night, and he developed a fever.

"You go on ahead of us and meet up with James," Aunt Tamsen urged Mama the next morning. "I need another day to tend to George."

Mama hesitated. "I'd rather travel with you," she said. Most likely she remembered the peril of traveling without our good friends.

"Charlie will be with us this time, Mama," I reminded her.

"And we'll be fine, Margaret. Heavens. There are more than twenty of us Donners, including our teamsters. You go on, now."

In the end, Mama's eagerness to see Pa won out. So we hugged all the Donners good-bye, and my family started the climb to Truckee Lake with the advance party.

TWENTY TWO

OCTOBER 1846. THE CLIMB.

All fifty-two members of our advance party followed the Truckee River up the zigzagging California Trail. Charlie hadn't exaggerated the difficulty of climbing the east side of the Sierra. The oxen strained to pull their lightened wagons up rocky slopes. Patty and Tommy kept their rides behind the Indian guides, but the uphill weight of both Charlie and me was too hard on Banjo, so every afternoon I got off to climb on foot while Charlie scouted ahead.

The days were a steady cold gray. Whenever I removed Milt's scarf from my nose and mouth, I could see my breath in the air, yet the effort of climbing the unyielding slopes made my body damp with sweat. Despite the chill, I ended up shedding my jacket each day. The trail was slippery; smooth rocks were embedded in the earth, and patches of soft gravel sometimes rolled underfoot. I kept my eyes on my boots as I picked my way around them.

Nights we camped against boulders or beneath ledges, warming ourselves by small fires and wrapping our bodies in quilts and buffalo robes. We pitched tents wherever we found room, and there was little conversation among us.

After three days of climbing, Truckee Lake was not in sight.

On the fourth morning we ascended through a freezing rain. Riding Banjo behind Charlie, I saw a white haze shrouding the peaks. "Is it snowing up there?" I asked him.

"Hard to tell," Charlie answered.

It wasn't the answer I wanted to hear. But I pushed away my fear. Instead, I imagined Pa and his relief party appearing around the next turn, and then the next. Maybe today would be the day I would see him.

On the fifth day the sun reappeared and warmed us, in between occasional dark clouds. The Truckee River abruptly dropped away to the south, and we ascended to Alder Creek, a level valley with tall pines and melting snowdrifts.

"Only five miles more to the lake," Charlie announced as we stopped to noon by the creek. Melting ice lined its banks. "We'll wait for the Donners once we get there."

The oxen and what was left of the other livestock grazed on half-frozen grasses. My family sat on the faded patchwork quilt that Aunt Lydia made us a lifetime ago. I ate a lunch of dried beef and water, then wandered off to rest beneath one of the more sheltered trees. I inhaled its strong, clean scent. I hoped the Donners were following by now. I missed talking to Leanna.

"We may already be in California territory." Mr. Breen's voice lifted above his family's conversation near their wagon.

Granite boulders. Groves of shadowy pines. Slushy mud. This wasn't the California I'd been promised. Where were the sun-filled valleys?

We finally reached the long, gray Truckee Lake just before sunset. The land surrounding it was flat and heavily forested with pines and firs so tall, I could barely see the sky when standing among them.

Last night's snow had melted from their branches, but the drifts were higher here. It must be snowing every night, I thought uneasily. I scanned the length of the lake to its opposite shore, where the summit peaks rose.

This was where our last long climb would begin.

Everyone set up tents, and I helped Mama start a campfire near the wall of a smooth granite rock. Before long my family—including Milt and Charlie, and now Luis and Salvador—was warming itself around it.

"See that shack?" Charlie pointed to a long, makeshift structure half buried by fallen branches. He pulled on his pipe. "Luis and Salvador told me it was built by a couple of pioneers stranded here two winters ago."

"That must be the very shack a trapper told us about at campfire one night on the plains," Mama said, handing Tommy a cup of water. "Imagine. The men spent almost two weeks stranded here waiting for the snow to melt."

Stranded. Here. For two whole weeks. I put my arm around Patty and pulled her closer. How could they bear it?

We ate a dinner of beans and bread, then settled into tents for the night, planning to stay until the Donners caught up.

"We have to get through the pass *now*. Otherwise we could be trapped here for weeks."

It was Charlie's voice.

I was barely awake when I opened the tent flap. A thin layer of new snow covered the ground. Charlie and Milt were strapping bags onto the pack mules. Mama, tight lipped, was pulling a knit cap over Tommy's head. Beyond us, Mr. Graves and some of the other men were hastily folding tents. When I looked past the lake, fear clawed my insides. Dark clouds shrouded the mountains.

I looked over my shoulder at Patty, who was blinking her eyes awake. Somehow we had both slept through the sudden surge of activity.

"Patty, get up," I whispered. "We're leaving!"

"Did the Donners get here already?"

"Not just yet. They'll catch up later."

But worries swirled through my mind as I sat behind Charlie along the foggy north shore. How would Leanna feel when she and her family reached the lake to find us gone? And shouldn't Pa have shown up by now?

Within two hours we were on the west side of the lake and starting our ascent. Progress was slow on the steep grade. Boots slipped on the icy trail; wagons creaked and rattled. The higher we climbed, the higher the snowdrifts, and soon only white surrounded us. By now the snow was well over the top of our boots, and we slowed until we simply stopped climbing. Luis and Salvador went ahead to check conditions at the pass.

The day was coming to an end, and we'd managed to climb only two miles beyond the lake. I helped Mama set up our tent using a cliff outcrop for shelter. Patty kept Tommy busy with nursery-rhyme tunes while little Cash, exhausted, slept beside them.

The Indian guides returned at dusk and reported to Charlie. Word spread through camp that deeper snows awaited us.

"It's a race against time now, Margaret," Charlie said as he crouched by the fire outside our tent. He rubbed his forehead a moment, then looked up. "If this weather continues, we have to reach the pass tomorrow."

My stomach clenched. *Or what?* But I didn't say anything. Patty and Tommy were still awake.

"What about the Donners?" Mama asked. They're at least a day behind us, maybe two."

I envisioned Leanna and all the little Donner children struggling through falling snow, trying to reach the summit. Tears sprang to my eyes.

Charlie shook his head. "We can only hope the pass stays clear long enough for all of us to get through," he said.

That night rain pounded our tent. Mama assured us that rain was a good thing. It would probably melt some of the snow. We awoke to a dry, gray sky, but there was fresh snowfall on the slopes above us. We started out at daybreak.

We had climbed only an hour when, despite yelling and threats and cracking of whips, the oxen would no longer pull through the deep drifts.

"Abandon the wagons," Charlie ordered. He walked among the families, his tone anxious. "Strap what you can to your animals."

Mrs. Graves protested loudly, but Mr. Graves, grim faced and determined, was already unhitching their oxen and pulling canvas bags from the broken-down wagons that had carried them so far.

"Mama, our things are in there!" I said, thinking of the extra clothing and blankets the Graveses had been carrying for us. Mama looked from the Graveses' wagon to the rocky crags of the summit. "Milt," she called out. "Pack whatever you can on your horse and the mule."

My family, with our pitifully reduced belongings, was quickly ready to move on, but we had to wait through at least another hour of tearful arguing while other families—those still with wagons and property—struggled over what to carry and what to leave behind.

The oxen weren't used to packing weight. Some tried to buck off their burdens. Others rolled on the ground in an effort to scrape them off. When the packs broke free and supplies scattered across the snow, men cursed and women wept in frustration. Another hour passed while the grownups tried to calm their oxen and salvage their remaining food.

When we resumed the climb I was first in line behind Charlie and the Indians. My boots seemed to sink deeper with every step as we led the mules and our one cow. Mama, carrying Cash, followed with Patty. Milt carried Tommy. By now most all the parents were carrying children through knee-high snow.

I gasped for breath. My clothing was soaked, my legs burned, and my feet felt like blocks of ice. But I willed myself to keep going: if I stopped, those behind me might stop too. "One foot in front of the other," I kept telling myself. "Pa is behind the next turn."

But when the wind picked up, the cold and exhaustion were too much to bear. Parents could no longer carry their children. Oxen were stumbling. Charlie called another halt.

"Rest here for a couple of hours," he said. "I'll go on ahead and check the pass." Then he disappeared on horseback with Luis and Salvador.

Some of the men chopped down a dead tree and lit it. It spit and crackled and burst into wind-whipped flames. I stood motionless as others moved around me. My body felt frozen through. My mind seemed to have stopped working.

"Puss." Mama tugged at my arm. "Sit down now. Wrap this quilt around you. Stay close to the fire."

I obeyed as she pulled the quilt over my head and tucked it around me.

The men threw more dead branches on the fire. I couldn't control my shaking as the heat penetrated my body.

Where was Pa? Probably very close. I would surely see him tomorrow. Maybe tonight.

Mama motioned for Patty and Tommy to lie down on the buffalo robe. Somewhere in the back of my mind, I knew I should be helping with the children. But I couldn't move my limbs, and my teeth were chattering. Around me, weary families huddled close to the fire, sinking into robes and blankets.

Time slipped by. There was no talking. Men continued to feed the flames. Most everyone else was asleep or, like me, staring blankly into the fire.

The men returned hours later. "We just finished marking the trail," Charlie said, his voice heavy with fatigue. "We're only three miles from the pass. But we have to get to it now, while it's still light."

Mr. Graves dumped another bundle of dead branches on the fire. "We're settled in now, Charlie," he said. "By the time we get up and moving, it'll be dark."

"Then we'll go in the dark," Charlie answered, his voice rising. I looked up from the fire in time to see him half fall from Banjo. "There's plenty of moonlight," he said, fighting for balance.

How could Charlie lead us through the pass? He could barely stand.

"My children are sleepin'," Mr. Breen said. "We'll go in the morning, when they're rested."

I'd never once seen Charlie lose his temper. But now his face turned dark. "Then your children must *be moved* through the pass. Don't you understand? If it snows again tonight, morning will be too late."

Mr. Keseberg, who'd also been feeding the flames, called out from the other side of the fire. "You're wrong. The sky is clearing, See the moon?"

I looked skyward. The full moon, surrounded by a halo of light, was floating in an open patch of dark-blue sky.

Charlie gave up on the men for the moment and approached Mama. The firelight glinted off his glasses as he crouched down. "Margaret," he urged. "You haven't traveled all this way to miss California by a day. Only three more miles. We can still make it to the summit. Your husband and his relief party are somewhere on the other side."

Mama didn't seem to hear him. She turned to me. "Lie down with the others, dear," she said, motioning toward the buffalo robe.

I rose and walked to where the children lay. They were wet, intertwined, and sound asleep. Little Cash slept in Tommy's arms. I sat beside them.

What about you, Mama? I tried to say. But my lips wouldn't move. The world around me had shrunk to only the darkening sky, the numbing cold, and the piercing wind.

Just beyond the fire the Indian Salvador stood beneath a tree. He'd wrapped himself in a blanket and appeared to be studying the moon. A wave of fear passed through me when snowflakes swirled around his body. I looked down at my lap. New flakes were falling on the buffalo robe. Defeated, I lay down next to Patty and drew it over my head.

In my dream I was still cold, even though it was summer and I was back on the plains. Billy was there, sleek and spirited, galloping through the tall grasses. The Sioux boy was astride him, bareback, his hands wound deep into Billy's mane.

"You found my pony," I cried out.

The boy reined Billy in and lifted his head. His eyes searched the horizon.

"Puss. Wake up." Charlie's voice.

The Sioux boy caught my eye and waved. Then he and Billy began to fade away.

"Don't go," I called.

Someone was shaking me. "I can't wake her." Mama's voice rose. "I can't wake her, Charlie!"

"Please don't go," I whispered.

Billy and the Sioux boy vanished.

The daylight hurt my eyes. Mama and Charlie were kneeling over me, their frightened faces close to mine. Between them, through snow-laden branches, I saw a gray-white sky. Morning.

"Did the snow stop?" I asked.

"Oh, thank God," Mama said. She slid her arm beneath my shoulders and gently sat me up.

I was alone in the buffalo-robe bed. The snow had created a thick blanket during the night. Women were digging frantically through drifts, looking for buried supplies. Men were prodding our spent oxen with sticks, forcing them to stand.

Everyone was moving in slow motion. Except for the distant sound of a woman weeping, the scene was eerily silent.

Mama hovered closer. "It took a long time to wake you," she said softly. She rubbed my arm as though to thaw me out.

Something inside me began to sink.

"Is everyone getting ready to go through the pass?"

Mama dropped her hand. She turned her head away.

"Charlie?" I said.

The answer was already in his face.

"No, Puss." His voice cracked. "The pass is closed. We're trapped."

TWENTY THREE

NOVEMBER 1846. TRAPPED.

With new energy fed by panic, we took less than a day to backtrack to the east end of Truckee Lake. The sky cleared a bit, and over the next few days the men axed pines and stacked thatched logs into windowless cabin walls. The roofs were made of thin branches laid close together and covered with oxhides. Ours was a two-room, two-family cabin divided by a center wall. Each side had a crude stone fireplace and an oxhide door. The Graves family settled in on the other side.

The Breens took possession of the partially collapsed shack left from two years before. Mr. Keseberg cursed in German as he worked alone to erect a lean-to alongside it for his own family. Two other families traveling with us, the Murphys and the Eddys, shared a cabin similar to ours. Big Bill McCutchen and his wife and baby moved in with the Eddys.

Missing the pass—and reuniting with Pa—by only one day was heartbreaking. And yet I was grateful for the snug cabin that was hardly bigger than the bedroom Patty and I had once shared in Springfield. It was warm and dry, and I hadn't slept inside anything but a wagon or tent for more than six months. I was grateful to have Charlie with us, too. Like Milt, he chopped wood, fetched water, and checked on the other families. But it was his high standing with the rest of the party that gave me a sense of safety I wouldn't have had otherwise. With Charlie in our cabin, Mr. Graves and Mr. Keseberg were unlikely to try anything mean.

The Donners, we learned, had made it only as far as Alder Creek, where they set up their own camp of twenty-two people. Knowing my family had lost nearly everything by now, they gave Milt items to carry back from his treks there: cups and dishes, flour and beans, an extra blanket or two, needles and yarns—and from Aunt Tamsen, storybooks for Patty and Tommy.

Milt killed our one cow, and Mama rationed its meat and what was left of the flour. She assured our expanded family—now including Luis and Salvador—that by eating one meal of dried beef or beans and baked biscuits a day, we'd have enough food for three weeks. It was unthinkable we'd be trapped here longer than that.

But each morning we woke to skies of cold, gray clouds and another night's snowfall weighing down branches, covering our roofs, and adding to the wall that blocked the pass. Most days those first weeks, I ventured out of the cabin with Patty or Tommy. We wouldn't wander far—to the lake's frozen shore, or to an icy meadow that allowed us to view the cruel beauty of the soaring granite cliffs and snow-laden forests that imprisoned us.

"When's Pa getting here?" Each time Tommy asked, which was at least once a day, I felt something catch in my chest. Pa and his relief party had surely been forced back to Sutter's Fort. Was he worried we'd run out of food, or did he assume we had enough cattle to keep us alive through the winter? He had no way of knowing the Piute had killed so many.

"The same snow that keeps us from getting to Pa keeps him from getting to us just now," I would answer. But then I'd find myself looking up at the summit as though expecting to see Pa on Glaucus, silhouetted against the sky.

Each night, it continued to snow.

Mama was determined to make our temporary living space more homelike.

"Girls, keep your blankets rolled up and stacked against the wall when we're not using them as beds," she instructed Patty and me. "Just because we're crowded doesn't mean we can't be orderly."

"You be sure to tell me whenever we get low on water in that bucket there, the one by the door," she told Tommy. He took his job to heart, peeking in the bucket several times a day and excitedly telling Milt when it was time to get more water.

She made Patty and me brush and rebraid our hair every single morning—something we hadn't had to do on the trail since leaving the plains. She even took to wearing her white house cap from Springfield as she warmed strips of meat or baked hard biscuits over the fire. And even though our table was Aunt Lydia's patchwork quilt spread across the frozen dirt floor, she insisted we all, even Luis and Salvador, say grace over our shrinking rations each day. Charlie followed Mama's example and spent the long hours after our meal leading songs or telling stories and encouraging us, even Patty and Tommy, to do the same.

After three weeks we were still trapped, and Mama stopped talking about somehow getting through the pass. When we ran out of meat, Mr. Breen gave us pieces of his slaughtered oxen.

Mama and I stood outside his shack, watching him lift the butchered cuts from a deep hole in the snow. The air was clear, but so cold I could barely stand still. I hugged myself and stomped in place, wishing he would hurry up.

"I promised your husband I'd take care of you and the children best I can, but I'm not responsible for the men stayin' in your cabin," he told Mama. "They'll have to look after themselves."

He handed the cuts, each about the size of a loaf of bread, to Mama and me.

"Who do you mean? Milt and Charlie?" Mama asked, furrowing her brow.

"And the Indians," Mr. Breen answered, his lips quivering slightly beneath his red mustache. "This here's enough to keep you and yer children fed a few more weeks."

Mama's cheeks flushed pink. "Why, Patrick," she said, her new boldness resurfacing. "Those Indians are Christians, same as you and me. And you're talking about Milt and Charlie as though they're strangers. Milt is like family, and Charlie— where would be all be without Charlie?"

Mr. Breen let her question hang a moment. Then his green eyes flashed. "Where would we be without Charlie?" he said, his brogue thickening. "We'd be on the other side of this mountain! Remember Truckee Meadows? How I wanted to start climbin' right away? Charlie talked us out of it!"

The Irishman's angry burst felt like a sharp slap. I took a step back, but Mama just shook her head.

"You're wrong about that, Patrick," she said quietly. "Think of all those days we wasted along the way. We both know there's plenty of blame to go around."

"Mama, let's go."

Mr. Breen pressed his lips together as he glanced at me. He turned back to Mama.

"Even so, Margaret, I'm givin' you and the children enough to get by for now. If you want to share with grown men and Indians, and deprive your own children, that's your business."

Mama stared at him in disbelief.

"Let's *go*, Mama," I said, my heart pounding. I turned and started back to the cabin. When I looked over my shoulder, Mama was following.

"Margaret," Mr. Breen called out after us. "I'm *sorry*. But I must think of my own family first."

Twenty Four

December 1846. Charlie.

Food. I thought about it all the time. Not just while waiting for my once-a-day meal, which I'd been doing for some time now, but in a larger, more frightening way. What would we do when this meat ran out? Would Mr. Breen give us more? What if he wouldn't? Would one of the other families help us?

During the fifth week it stopped snowing for three nights in a row. The fourth morning, Charlie and the Indian guides optimistically bundled up, packed a few days' rations, and started out on foot for the summit.

"We won't be taking food from your mouths anymore," Charlie said as he adjusted the pack on his back. He grinned good-naturedly at the small group that had gathered to wish him luck. "In fact, we'll be bringing food back."

His manner was so convincing I was certain our long wait might soon be over. But the men returned to camp that very afternoon, exhausted and shivering with cold.

Once inside the cabin, Luis and Salvador hurried toward the hearth to warm up as Charlie dropped his pack and sagged in the doorway. His trousers were soaked stiff all the way to his waist. "It's at least ten feet deep up there," he told us, removing his glasses and wiping them on his sleeve. "Much worse than when we turned back last month."

His failure to reach the pass that day turned out to be a blessing. That very same night another storm swirled in, this one howling for four days and nights, piling new snowdrifts throughout camp. Milt scraped snow from our hearth every morning. When the storm finally ended, he dug a sloped tunnel from our door into the daylight. Patty and I ventured out.

The flakey white powder half buried our cabins and climbed the lower trunks of the trees. It glistened in the bright sunlight, making us squint. A man, I thought, could easily get lost in these drifts. A small child could completely disappear.

"Puss. Look." Patty's eyes lit up. She grabbed my hand and pointed.

I hadn't seen the lake in full sunlight until now. It was frozen sky-blue and mirrored the uncaring grandeur of the surrounding peaks. Its beauty nearly took my breath away.

But the grownups didn't notice; scores of them milled around the center of camp, talking in low voices. They looked up at the summit, looked away, and looked up again with expressions of dismay.

It was now far too dangerous to wander off, and the men's treks to Alder Creek to check on the Donners all but stopped. Mr. Breen must have forgotten his reluctance to feed Charlie and the Indians, because he gave us more meat. Mama cut it into tiny pieces and boiled it with beans to make it stretch.

We were almost always in our cabins now, and we lost all notion of time as the days slid by, each a pale shadow of the one before. More storms buried us, and party members burrowed in like prairie dogs, taking long naps during the day. Our cabin stayed warm—sometimes too warm—from our body heat. I spent my few waking hours reading aloud to Tommy from the children's books Milt had carried back from the Donner camp. Luckily, Tommy was young enough to want to hear them over and over again. Other times I made up stories about the ponies he and Patty were going to get in California, or joined him in games of fetch and tug-of-war with little Cash.

Milt and Charlie told stories, too. Hour after hour, I'd lie on my stomach near the hearth, hands under my chin, and listen to the two men spin long, detailed descriptions of farming their own land or starting their own businesses. I wondered: Had Pa claimed our California land yet? Maybe, since he couldn't get to us, he was building a house, getting everything ready for when he could come back and rescue us.

Mama read Bible passages aloud and often led us in prayer. We bent our heads, asking for our safety and the safety of our friends. For it to stop snowing. For Pa to appear.

Thy will be done, we all said.

All of us except Charlie.

"Why don't you pray with us, Charlie?" I asked him one night. "Don't you believe in God?"

"In a sense I do, Puss." He smiled through his scanty beard, but his eyes were serious. "I don't say prayers or go to church to find him. He's already here—in the winds, the birds, and animals—even the snowfall. I feel him in nature."

I remembered my fear at the fierce power of the Kansas River, my awe at the vast flocks of migrating birds on the plains, and the thrill of riding Billy through the Rockies. And surely only God could shape the mysterious formation of Chimney Rock. Even here at the lake, whenever the sun came out, the snowfall that bent the pine boughs and buried our cabins glittered like fallen stars.

So in a way I understood him. But in another way I didn't. Did Charlie think all our prayers were in vain? I was afraid of his answer, so I didn't ask. We had run out of flour, and we were running out of meat again. Prayers were all we had left.

In mid-December there was another break in the weather. Charlie, Mr. Graves and his daughter Mary, the Indian guides, and twelve other party members gathered under a clear blue sky. Each packed a week's worth of food and wore snowshoes that Charlie and Mr. Graves had fashioned from oxbows and rawhide.

The group christened themselves the Forlorn Hope. They were bound for Sutter's Fort, and their departure was both welcomed and dreaded by those of us left behind. Welcomed, because what remained of our food would last longer with seventeen fewer people in camp. Dreaded, because if they failed to reach Sutter's Fort and get help, we would surely die here.

I struggled with my feelings as I watched Charlie tie on his snowshoes. Of course he had to try. We'd been trapped here forty-five days. He and the Indian guides were the only men who could lead the others across the Sierra. I'd said good-bye to him so many times that it should be easier by now. But this time was harder than ever. It was his presence in our cabin—his sure manner, his hopeful conversation, his even temperament—that had kept my family's fears from spiraling out of control these horrible weeks. How would Mama and I hang on with him gone?

"Puss, keep something for me, would you?" he asked me as he dug through his pack, his expression intent. "My brother's wife in New York—I gave her a ruby pin on her twenty-first birthday." He pulled out a small cloth bag and handed it to me.

"She sent it to me when my business failed. She wanted me to sell it and keep the money. But it was a gift! I'm going to return it when I get settled."

He raised his eyes. "Keep it for me?" he asked again. "I don't want to lose it in the snow."

He could have asked Mama to keep it, but he had asked me. Warmth flooded my face as I slid the round ruby pin from the bag into my palm. I lowered my head and pretended to study its delicate shape, but this time my color gave me away.

"Virginia."

I looked up. Charlie's eyes shone behind his glasses.

"You're the bravest young woman I know. You belong in California. I know you'll get there. We'll meet again at Sutter's Fort, if not before."

Hours later, long after the Forlorn Hope had disappeared over the summit, I realized Charlie had called me a woman.

TWENTY FIVE

JANUARY-FEBRUARY 1847. WAITING.

N ow weeks, not days, slid by. A steady, gnawing ache inside kept me awake day and night, my mind spinning
with memories of home. Springfield. It was all so long ago. Did
Mary remember me? Did she wonder why she'd stopped hearing from me? If I could send her a letter, what would I say?
That Mrs. Graves agreed to sell Mama four cattle, but only after
Mama signed a paper that she'd pay double their worth when
we got to California. That Mama was so angry she started shaking, and when she realized Mrs. Graves had sold us her skinni-
est ones, she cried. That Milt tried to hunt small game, but no
animals were to be found. That Ed Breen and some other boys
broke through the ice near shore and tried to fish, but had no
luck.

Milt, partly bored and partly worried, ignored Mama's
pleadings not to leave and walked the six miles to the Donner
camp through the deep drifts. "They're worse off than we are,
Mrs. Reed," he said when he returned the next afternoon. The
firelight framed his thinning profile. Normally lean, he now
looked like a stick figure as he sat by the hearth and crossed his
legs. "George Donner's hand never healed. He's fevered and
bedridden, and so is his brother Jake. And they've no meat left

at all." He paused a moment, his mouth working. "The children are eating glue boiled from cowhide."

"Oh, no," Mama said faintly, as though listening from far away, and her face blanched. I imagined Leanna and her sisters trying to swallow the rancid goo. My stomach contracted in disgust.

"And the teamsters," Milt continued. "The teamsters are eating whatever wood mice they can catch."

I glanced anxiously at the children, hoping they hadn't heard. But Patty and Tommy were sleeping soundly near the wall, little Cash between them.

Later that night, while Mama prayed for the Donners, I bent my head and touched the rosary necklace beneath my bodice.

"Virginia, you don't have to hide that from me anymore," Mama said softly.

I looked up, startled. How long had she known I was wearing it? But Mama's head stayed bent, and she continued to pray aloud. I pulled the beads out from my collar and held the crucifix while I prayed under my breath.

"Holy Mary, Mother of God, pray for us sinners…"

The next morning a two-day storm hit camp. It was followed by another, and then another. When Milt finally dug up through the tunnel into daylight, he discovered the remaining two cattle Mama bought from Mrs. Graves were missing—buried by the snow.

Would Mary believe me if I wrote her we were cutting pieces of hide from our roof and boiling them? That we were reduced to eating the soupy goo it made, same as the Donners? That Milt spent hours each day poking long sticks in the snow, hopelessly trying to find our buried cattle?

The gnawing ache in my stomach had turned to sharp, knife-like pains that sometimes shot out to my arms and legs. And every evening, before my ration of the wretched glue, I felt a belt tightening around my forehead. I was finding it harder to care about anything but my next chance to eat.

The hunger was worse for Tommy, who didn't understand why his insides hurt so much. He continually asked Mama for bread. But Patty, who sometimes couldn't keep the glue down, seemed to be suffering the most—her very face was shrinking.

One morning Mrs. Graves crawled down our sloped tunnel to tell us she heard that Uncle Jacob and three Donner teamsters had starved to death at Alder Creek. Mama, who was helping Tommy sketch on the stone hearth with burnt sticks, steered the woman out before she could say anything more.

"It's absolutely not true," Mama assured us as she turned back from the door. But her face was white as I've ever seen it.

That same evening she roused us from our half sleep, half stupor, telling us she had found more meat. Patty stared into the pot for a long time before asking Mama where Cash was. Mama looked down and shook her head. Patty's mouth twitched, as though she was trying to decide whether or not to cry. I looked from her to Mama, then ladled a little chunk out, sat down, and ate it with my bare hands. After a while Patty and Tommy asked for meat, too.

For three days we lived on our little pet, gratefully eating every bit of him we could swallow.

With Cash gone, we truly had nothing else to eat. We'd already torn as much hide from the roof as we could without it collapsing in on us. So the Breens took my family in, and the Graveses made room for Milt on their side of the cabin.

"I can't give your family any of our meat," Mr. Breen explained to Mama and me. His brogue was thick with misery. "I have to think of my family first." But he did give us two hides, and Mrs. Breen gave us bones to boil for broth.

The Breens weren't nearly as weak as we'd become, and Tommy and Patty both perked up briefly in the company of the active Breen children. Ed and his younger brothers rarely seemed to run out of talk or indoor games.

Mr. Breen read passages from the Bible aloud to us twice each day, and he also led his family in a daily prayer from the Rosary. Mama didn't object when Mrs. Breen showed me the right way to hold my necklace, which she called prayer beads, as I listened.

Christ hear us.
Christ graciously hear us.

The days continued to drag by. Mrs. Graves arrived at the Breen cabin and asked for Mama and me. She told us she couldn't wake Milt, and we had to come get him. I could scarcely breathe as we followed the woman down her tunnel and through her door. Milt was lying on the floor, so thin and gray I didn't recognize him. Mama knelt and shook him, crying out, "He starved to death! He starved to death!" while Mrs. Graves and her children looked on.

I burst into tears. Why hadn't Milt moved in with us? He'd still be alive!

"He's your responsibility now, Margaret," Mrs. Graves said.

I knelt next to Mama, shaking her arm. "Let's take him. Let's take him out of here."

We pushed and pulled Milt's body up the Graveses' sloped tunnel by ourselves. By the time we reached daylight we were too exhausted to bury him, so we sat next to his body and covered him with handfuls of snow, starting with his stocking-covered feet and working up. Mama prayed under her breath the entire time. She couldn't bring herself to cover his face, so I patted snow over his mouth and nose and around his ears and eyes, sobbing as I whispered good-bye. Then, numb with cold and grief, Mama and I stumbled back to the Breen cabin and slept.

February arrived. By now all of us, even the Breens, spent our days drifting in and out of sleep, passively waiting for rescue. Mr. Breen said the Forlorn Hope must have reached Sutter's Fort weeks ago. Shouldn't help be on the way? Now and then, when the sun broke through the overcast sky, I took Patty or Tommy up to the snow that covered the Breen roof and watched the summit, hoping to see Charlie or Pa or anyone walking toward us carrying food.

One late afternoon Patty and I sat on the roof to get away from the heat and smell in the cabin. The trees cast slender shadows throughout camp. Directly above us, a light snow began to fall.

"Look, Puss."

I turned to Patty. Her little face was upturned. She closed her eyes and smiled as the falling flakes melted on her cheeks and eyelids. "Angel kisses," she said.

A shiver ran through my body. When was the last time we'd eaten? Two days ago? Three?

Because Patty wasn't smiling. The setting sun was angled on her paper-thin skin, making it transparent. I was seeing her skull-like teeth through closed lips.

That night I fought to stay awake. It was hard; my thoughts kept drifting off to strange places. But I believed if I let sleep overtake me, Patty, who slept beside me, might never wake up.

All my prayers for rescue hadn't worked. What was God waiting for?

I fingered the rosary necklace. Was God waiting for me to become a Catholic? I had promised Pa I wouldn't. But Patty was dying. We were all dying.

I left Patty's side and dizzily fell to my knees on the frozen dirt floor. I pressed the tiny crucifix between my palms and promised God I would become a Catholic if he would save my family and let me see Pa again. I knelt there for a very long time until gradually, the peace I'd been longing for so long returned.

TWENTY SIX

FEBRUARY 1847. VOICES.

"I saw Grandma last night."

I was awakened by Patty's breath in my ear.

Daylight poured down through the chimney, lighting the hearth with a hazy glow.

"Hush, Patty. Everyone's sleeping."

"I did." Patty propped herself on one elbow. Her skin was dead white, her dark eyes unfocused.

"It was a dream."

"No, it wasn't. She talked to me. She—"

"Hush."

Patty's voice fell back to a whisper. "She said she's watching over us from heaven."

I glanced over at Mama. I didn't want her to see Patty like this. "Stay here and be quiet."

I crept closer to the hearth and knelt beside Mrs. Breen. The woman's green eyes were wide open. She seemed to be staring through the ceiling.

"Mrs. Breen—"

"Do you hear voices, lass?" she asked without turning.

"No." I paused a moment, confused. "Mrs. Breen, can you give Patty something to eat?"

Mrs. Breen peered upward a moment more and pushed her blankets aside. "Someone's outside."

Then she was on her feet. I called after her as she disappeared out the door. "Wait!"

Was Mrs. Breen going mad, like Patty?

"Praise be to God," I heard her shout. "Are you men from California, or do you come from heaven?"

Mama lifted her head. "What's that commotion?" she asked.

"Just Mrs. Breen," I said.

"No." Mama said. "I hear men's voices." She sat up for a moment, her expression intent. Then she pulled a quilt over her shoulders and followed Mrs. Breen up the tunnel.

Now I heard the voices, too. What was going on up there? I was too tired to crawl up the tunnel just now. I walked back to Patty and sat down. She had already gone back to sleep.

"Puss. *Puss!*" I opened my eyes.

Mama was kneeling over me. Her face was drained of color, as though she'd seen a ghost. "They made it to Sutter's Fort."

"Charlie's here?" I sat up so fast the room spun. "Is he outside?"

"No. They say he's recovering from frostbite. But there's a relief party outside." Her voice began to quiver. "And they say your father is close behind with another one."

Pa? My heart raced. Pa was close by! As I hugged Mama, I saw that the cabin was nearly empty. Most everyone must have left while the children and I slept.

Patty and Tommy stayed in the cabin while I followed Mama into the daylight, gasping for breath in the cold air. When my eyes adjusted to the light I saw seven men huddled together in the center of camp, their eyes wide.

Other party members emerged from the surrounding cabins, and for a brief moment I saw what our rescuers saw—gaunt, ghastly beings rising from the depths. Some were weeping, others laughing as they stumbled toward the men.

But we were saved. We were going to live. Last night's vow to become a Catholic had hastened our rescue. I was sure of it.

Four of the men began handing out small quantities of bread. The other three, upon hearing about the Donner camp, hurried on to Alder Creek.

"Please," I said to the tired-eyed man who gave me a small, unleavened square. "I need more. I have a sister and brother who can't leave the cabin."

He eyed me suspiciously. "It's not safe to eat too much at one time, young lady."

But Mama convinced the man, whose name was Mr. Glover, to give us bread for Patty and Tommy. As we started back toward the cabin with our rations, I heard him say to a fellow rescuer, "Another day and we would have been too late."

"We're already too late for some," the other man said. "Ten have already died in this camp alone, I'm told."

Mama and I exchanged looks. Ten dead? He must be wrong.

Patty gained enough strength from the small squares of bread to be clear-eyed the following morning, but she was still too weak to leave the cabin. Tommy followed me into the sunshine. He shyly touched our rescuers as though he needed reassurance the men were real.

That evening Mr. Glover called Mama and me over. He said Pa's relief party was due in a week and a third relief party would arrive a week or so after that.

"We have only enough food stashed along the trail for thirty people, including ourselves," he explained. "Since you have no food to hold you over until your husband gets here, I want you to leave with us tomorrow."

Mama turned to me. "Then we'll see your father on the trail." A sob escaped her, and her hand flew to her mouth.

"Puss!" The voice was familiar. I turned.

The three rescuers who had gone on to Alder Creek were herding a group of scrawny children toward us. One of them, a girl about my height, waved.

"It's me—Leanna," she called.

Four months had gone by since I'd seen Leanna. This girl had her voice, but didn't look like her.

"Oh, my stars, Puss. You're so skinny," the girl said as she got closer.

Then she smiled.

"It *is* you." I held out my arms and we managed a bony embrace. Leanna's heart was pounding beneath the ribs.

"We just found out we're leaving tomorrow," I said, studying her shrunken face. "Are you coming with us?"

"Just us." Leanna gestured to a sister and Aunt Betsy's son Will. "The others are staying with my parents until your pa gets here. Papa's arm isn't any better and—" Leanna's voice trailed off and she looked away. Mama put a hand on her shoulder.

The next morning twenty-three party members, including my family, Ed Breen and one of his brothers, and Mrs. Keseberg and her little girl, prepared to leave camp with Mr. Glover and his men. Most were children, and nearly all of us, even little Tommy, were going to have to walk. This time their parents were too weak to carry them.

"Surely one of you men can help me carry Ada," Mrs. Keseberg said as she juggled her three-year-old daughter in her arms.

"Sorry, ma'am," Mr. Glover said. "She'll have to walk. We'll be ahead scraping and packing down snow."

He and the other rescuers moved forward and we party members followed. As we ascended the slope, I recalled the first time we'd attempted the climb, last October. We were cold to the bone, carrying children and supplies, and trying to control the few oxen we had left. I thought I'd see Pa at any moment. And then the pass was blocked.

This time was different. The drifts might be deeper, but the sun was shining, and the branches were free of snow. This time we had rescuers to lead us. And this time I knew I would see Pa. God had answered the first part of my prayer; he would surely answer the second.

But we'd trekked only a few miles when I noticed my family was falling behind. Like the others, we climbed the slope by stepping into the boot marks of our rescuers, but Tommy's little legs didn't stretch that far. Holding hands with Mama, he tried to keep up by placing his knee on the little hill of snow between each mark and climbing over, while Mama encouraged him.

Patty and I followed. She was struggling to keep up, too, and several times I had to stop and wait for her.

My heart sank when I saw Mr. Glover walking down the slope toward us. His gloves were caked with snow from scraping the trail. He took Mama aside and spoke to her in a low voice.

"No," I heard Mama say. "She's doing fine. And I'll carry him if I have to."

Mr. Glover removed his gloves and slapped them against his leg to get the snow off. "They can stay with the Breens until your husband gets there. They'll be stronger by then."

"The Breens won't feed my children." Mama's voice rose. "They have barely enough for their own."

Tommy, hearing that, began to wail.

"I'll leave a week's supply of food for them," Mr. Glover said, lowering his voice. "And if your husband doesn't show up within a week, I'll go back for them myself."

By now the other rescuers and party members had stopped climbing. Some gathered around Mama and Mr. Glover.

"Say no, Mama." I looked down the slope at Patty. She was standing very still, her expression unreadable. For the first time in months, I thought of old Hardcoop's fate.

"Patty," I called out. "We're not going to leave you behind. I promised, remember?"

Patty nodded, but she was watching Mama.

Mama's eyes were wide with panic. "I won't send my babies back alone. We'll go back as a family and wait for James."

Mr. Glover's face darkened. "Your older daughter is strong enough to get out now, and so are you."

This couldn't be happening. I approached Mr. Glover. "Then just I will go back with them."

"I won't allow that," Mr. Glover said.

I put my hand on his arm. "I promised I wouldn't leave her," I whispered.

"It's all right," a little voice said. Everyone turned. There was something grown-up in Patty's resigned expression. "We'll go back and wait."

"Mama, we can't—"

But Mama was staring down at Mr. Glover's hand. "Mr. Glover, are you a Mason?"

He threw back his shoulders. "Why yes, ma'am, I am."

I studied his silver ring. It had the same insignia as Pa's Master Mason medal.

"So is my husband." Mama looked up, searching his face. "James and I put great store in the Masons." She glanced back at Patty before facing Mr. Glover again. "Do you give me your word, as a Mason, that if we don't meet up with James soon, you'll go back to the camp for his children?"

Mr. Glover stood ramrod straight. "I give you my word as a Mason," he said solemnly.

What was she doing? "No, Mama! Please! We can't leave them."

But Mama took Tommy's hand and walked down the slope toward Patty. She crouched next to both children, speaking in low tones. Patty nodded slowly. Tommy's cries quieted into soft hiccups.

Saying good-bye to Patty and Tommy was the hardest good-bye yet—even harder than saying good-bye to Pa. Tommy was stiff and unresponsive when I hugged him. I squeezed Patty's bird-like body as hard as I dared.

"I'm sorry I broke my promise," I said, hearing my voice crack.

Patty pulled away. Her little face looked old and tired. "You couldn't help it, Puss."

When Mama knelt for a final hug, Patty patted her shoulder. "If you don't see me again, Mama, then do the best you can."

Mama's back shook with sobs.

"Oh! But Patty," I heard myself say. "We'll see you soon. Real soon."

Mr. Glover had to turn his face away. But only minutes later he was leading Patty and Tommy down the slope and back to the lake camp.

I stood beside Mama and, as though in a dream, watched them go. Tommy kept turning around to wave, and I waved back each time. Patty never looked back. Mama stood frozen, unable to move or speak, until they rounded a corner and disappeared.

One day later we were on the other side of the summit. Mr. Glover caught up with us, assuring Mama that Patty and Tommy were sheltered safely with the Breens. But Pa hadn't appeared, and Mama was already regretting her decision.

"What have I done?" she asked me. "Oh, Puss, what have I done?"

Mama's remorse was frightening to watch. Each day she grew quieter. She began to walk with slow, sluggish steps. Eventually Leanna and I walked alongside her, each holding an arm and encouraging her to keep up.

The deepest snowdrifts were behind us. The sky was clear. We were safe now, but what did it matter? Pa was somewhere ahead of us. Patty and Tommy were back at the lake camp. Mama was right beside me, yet her mind was drifting away. Was this how God intended to answer my prayer?

On the fifth day as we crossed a westward ridge, I heard shouting ahead. I squinted in the sunlight. Three men were walking toward us. One called out, "Is Mrs. Reed with you?"

Mama's head snapped up, and the blood drained from her face.

"Yes," Mr. Glover yelled out. "And one of her children, also."

"Tell her that her husband is right behind us," the man called back. "He wanted her to know."

Mama cried out, then clumsily sank to the frozen ground, where she sat in a stupor.

"Mama." I pulled her to her feet as Leanna steadied her. Others rushed over to help. As soon as Mama was in good hands, I couldn't help myself—I let go and ran.

"Pa! Pa! Pa!" I yelled his name over and over, so he would know I was coming. My boots crunched on the packed snow.

Then, just as I had imagined, there he was in a turn of the trail. A blur of men and animals was behind him, but my eyes were only on the unkempt, skinny man who was striding ahead, leading a stocky brown horse.

"Puss!" Pa knew me the instant before I slammed into his arms. His beard was long and stiff, and his blistered lips scratched my cheek. I wanted to cling to him forever, but he called out Mama's name and released me. Moments later I was watching my parents embrace.

Rescuers and party members stopped to watch the reunion. I couldn't hear what my parents said, but I could tell when Pa learned about Patty and Tommy. He drew back and furrowed his brow.

"Too weak to continue!" His voice was audible again. His eyes searched the scattered crowd for Mr. Glover.

"How long will it take us to get there?" Pa asked when he spotted him.

"Four days, if the weather holds," Mr. Glover answered. "But hurry, Mr. Reed. They're very low on food."

My heart caught in my throat as Pa hurriedly straightened the pack on his horse. Only minutes had passed since, after months of waiting, I'd finally seen him walking toward me. Now I was watching him leave again. I would go on to Sutter's Fort with Mama while Pa hurried in the opposite direction—this time to save Patty and Tommy.

TWENTY SEVEN

FEBRUARY 1847. CALIFORNIA.

I stood on a turn of a muddy trail that looked onto the Sacramento Valley. Mr. Glover pointed southwest. Sixty miles away, he said, below the curve of a wide, dark river, Sutter's Fort sat on the valley floor.

We were a day below the snowline on a downward slope marked by oak trees and golden poppies. This was the California I had imagined.

Although a spring rain pattered on the wide-brimmed hat Milt had given me, sunrays now and then broke through the clouds to light the scene below. Low, gentle hills lay in the distance. Somewhere beyond that, Mr. Glover said, was the great Pacific Ocean.

Four days had passed since we met up with Pa. Not all the party members had made it this far. The little Keseberg girl died from the cold, and Leanna's cousin Will gorged on stolen bread and died when his weakened body couldn't digest it.

I wiped my eyes. "It's pretty as they all said, isn't it, Mama."

Mama nodded listlessly. The fort meant food, clean clothes, and people who would help us. Charlie would be waiting, as would the other members of the Forlorn Hope, expecting to greet the loved ones they left behind. But Pa, Patty, and Tommy were still in the mountains, and if it was raining down here, it was snowing up there. Had Pa reached Truckee Lake before this latest snowfall? Was he trapped at the lake camp with Patty and Tommy? Or worse, were the three of them part way down the mountain with no shelter when the storm hit?

I put my arm around Mama's waist. "If Pa made it here once, with all that's happened, he'll make it here again."

Mr. Glover gestured toward a grove of pines about twenty feet away. He asked that just the grownups follow. The children slumped to the ground where they stood, thankful for a chance to rest.

Leanna stayed with her sister and the other children, but I wanted to hear what our rescuer had to say. I grabbed Mama's hand and pulled her along with me.

"There's something I must tell you before you get to Sutter's Fort," Mr. Glover said, as we gathered around. He looked grim and a bit frightened.

"All winter we knew you were trapped, but we didn't know how serious your situation was. Most of us were down south fighting the war, and—"

"The war?" someone asked.

"Why, yes," Mr. Glover answered. "Right here in California. We're at war with Mexico."

We stood in confused silence, waiting for him to continue.

"As anxious as we were to get to you, we thought you'd be able to live off your livestock until the spring snowmelt. We had no way of knowing you'd lost so many..."

Mr. Glover paused so long that I thought he'd forgotten what he wanted to say.

"It wasn't until a man showed up at an outpost called Johnson's Ranch that we found out you were starving at the lake. He was little more than a skeleton, barely alive. He said others were a few miles back, unable to walk any farther."

He paused for another long time. "You see," he said, "we didn't want to tell you what happened to your friends you call the Forlorn Hope before now. We thought if you knew, you might not have the will to go on."

He took a long breath. "Only seven got through."

Only seven? A vise gripped my insides. *Charlie.*

"Mr. Stanton was the first to die."

Mama gasped.

"No, *no!*" I cried out. I covered my face in disbelief as Mr. Glover described how Charlie had become snow-blind from sun reflecting off the glittering snow.

His glasses. Tears streamed through my fingers.

"Mr. Stanton urged the others to hurry on without him, promising to catch up by nightfall. They left him alone at a campfire, peacefully smoking his pipe."

Then Mr. Glover's voice fell so low I could barely hear him. "He never left that campfire. We found him on our way up to you. He was frozen, his pipe still in his mouth. We buried him in the snow."

Somehow Leanna had arrived at my side. Her arms were around me, and we were both sobbing.

With Charlie dead, Mr. Glover continued, the Forlorn Hope lost their way. Eventually there was no food at all. One by one, beginning with Mr. Graves, they began to die. No food at all, he repeated. Only—I lifted my head from Leanna's shoulder and strained to hear—only the bodies of the dead.

Then Mr. Glover described what the living were forced to do to survive.

At first I thought I heard him wrong. He was talking about people eating people.

I gripped Leanna's arm as we listened in silent horror.

As Charlie had once told me, people in California were kind-hearted and generous. At Sutter's Fort we were given lamb and peas and cornbread, and we slept indoors in warm beds of hides and blankets. Captain Sutter himself came by to pay his respects, and sympathetic settlers' wives brought us clean clothes and hairbrushes. We washed in heated water and burned our filthy rags. Mama and I were given a room of our own, with a table and a cooking fireplace. Leanna and her sister, as well as most other members of our relief party, were sent to nearby farms.

The long days passed—three, five, seven—yet Mama and I were suspended in time. Each evening she sat near the fireplace, silently turning the pages of our family Bible as I cooked supper and tried to push away the incomprehensible: Pa, Patty, Tommy—and in a way, Mama—were they all lost to me?

Each day Mama stood watch at the fortress gate, looking east as I aimlessly roamed the grounds.

Sutter's Fort was even bigger than Fort Laramie. The eighteen-foot-high adobe walls encircled houses, stores, a blacksmith shop, a bakery, and several warehouses. Few men were about; most were down south fighting the war with Mexico. Women, Indians, old men, and children made up most of the population. All were kind, but I sometimes felt them watching me curiously. Many had heard about cannibalism in the mountains. Did these people think I had eaten human flesh?

After a few days, I rarely left our room.

On the tenth night, after Mama gave up her post at the gate and I cooked over our iron stove, I heard an old man shouting outside our door. The shouts got louder, and then there was an insistent pounding.

"Mrs. Reed! Your husband and both your children—they're on horseback, riding through the gate!"

TWENTY EIGHT

MAY 1847. HOME.

Pa had been talking about our new land for weeks. He had claimed it last December, while separated from us by the Sierra snows.

After leaving Sutter's Fort, we first moved in with the Sinclairs, a middle-aged couple who lived in nearby Napa Valley. We gained weight rapidly; my face was rounder each time I peeked into the hall mirror. Patty and Tommy spent most of their time playing outdoors on the Sinclairs' vast property. I stayed inside; I helped Mrs. Sinclair and Mama in the kitchen, listened to the men talk about the Mexican War, read books from the Sinclairs' library, cried alone in my room. I spent days writing a long letter to Mary describing our ordeal from beginning to end, and then asked Mr. Sinclair if he could find a way to send it to Springfield.

"Of course, my dear," he said. "I can take it into Sacramento. Someone I know recently started a mail-courier business there. He'll see that your letter is delivered."

A third relief party returned from the Sierra to Sutter's Fort. Pa took Mama and me aside and told us that the entire Breen family had survived. But Uncle George was found dead at the Alder Creek camp. So was Aunt Betsy. Aunt Tamsen had simply vanished.

After many questions and tears, Pa told us that rescuers claimed they'd found signs of cannibalism in both camps.

"Why, James, you know that simply isn't possible." Mama said, glancing nervously at me.

But I remembered all too well how we had eaten little Cash to stay alive, and what Mr. Glover had told us about the Forlorn Hope.

Anything could happen out there. Anything.

Our new land was a hundred miles south of Napa Valley. One morning in May, when we were all strong enough, we started the last leg of our journey—to a little settlement called San Jose.

We traveled in a borrowed open wagon pulled by borrowed mules, using borrowed money—all lent to Pa by California Masons. We'd lost everything we once owned, but Pa said we could start over. We were in California now. We were rich with opportunity.

Tommy sat in back, chattering loudly and playing with his new brown puppy. Patty sat beside them, fussing with the little doll that old Hardcoop had made for her. She had secretly dropped it in her deep dress pocket after Mama told her to leave it behind.

When she confessed to the doll after reaching Sutter's Fort, Mama held her for a long time. "I'm grateful you kept that little doll to comfort you those terrible months," she said.

I wanted to tell Pa how my rosary necklace had comforted me during those terrible months, but I suspected my confession wouldn't get the same loving reaction.

The southward trail led us to a wide canyon bordered by low mountains. Thick clumps of blue wildflowers and swatches of yellow mustard grew randomly among oaks and towering redwoods.

"If it were up to me," I said, sitting between my parents on the driver's bench, "I'd forget about going to San Jose. I would stay right here in the Napa Valley. This is even prettier than the Great Plains."

Pa smiled and brought the wagon to a halt. "We're not going to stay here. But we can have lunch here."

Pa stood behind Mama and put his hands on her shoulders as she sliced bread and fresh peaches. They were nearly inseparable these days.

"I'm going to eat over there," I said, grabbing my plate and pointing to a nearby creek bordered by willows.

But my food went untouched. I settled myself on a flat rock, closed my eyes, and listened to the water flow through the creek bed. A soft breeze cooled my face.

A year ago I left Springfield. A year ago I stood in the road beside Billy, closed my eyes just like this, and listened for the familiar sounds of home.

I lost so many loved ones while trying to reach this beautiful place. Grandma. Milt. Billy. I drew a long breath. Charlie.

California *ought* to be beautiful, I'd said in my letter to Mary, for all we left behind in getting here.

And I lost something else. Maybe it was a way of looking at the world. A way of looking at my parents. I was closer to them than ever before, and yet I'd grown away from them.

What would their lives be like here in California? Different, most likely, from what they imagined back in Springfield. And my own life? Much different, surely, from what they imagined for me.

Pa found me gazing through sunlight on water. "There you are," he said. "We'll be leaving soon." He pointed to my untouched plate. "Aren't you hungry?"

I shook my head. "Look, Pa. See those little minnows behind that row of rocks? They keep swimming back and forth, and just when you think they can't get through, you see one on the other side, swimming downstream. See? There goes another one."

Pa sat down beside me. He pulled off his hat and pushed back his hair. "Well, I'll be," he said. "I wonder how they do that."

"I bet Charlie would know."

A cloud passed over Pa's face as he scanned our surroundings. "Charlie would have loved it here." He paused. "Milt, too."

We sat in somber silence, watching the movement of the water.

Was this the time to tell him? I touched the rosary necklace beneath my bodice. It was going to take all the bravery I could muster. But if I could make him understand how the rosary had comforted me during our crossing, how it had strengthened me throughout our entrapment, and how it had brought him back into our lives, I could surely make him understand why I was going to break my promise to him and become a Catholic.

I took a deep breath. "Pa," I started.

Pa's brief melancholy fell away. He turned to me, eyes expectant, expression hopeful—like last year, when we started our journey.

My heart wavered. This wasn't the time to tell him, after all. I searched for something else to say.

"Pa, let's not go any farther. Let's stay right here."

Pa pushed himself up from the rock and looked around.

"This *is* a beautiful spot," he said. But he held out his hand and pulled me to my feet.

"Just a little farther, Virginia. We're almost there."

And then we went on.

EPILOGUE

B efore the railroads, even before the California Gold Rush, the members of the Donner Party were among the first emigrant families to cross the frontier to California. Out of eighty-seven men, women, and children, only forty-six survived. Two-thirds of the women and children made it to California. Two-thirds of the men perished, including Captain Sutter's Indian employees, Luis and Salvador. The only families to survive intact were the Reeds and the Breens.

Sensationalism was alive and well in 1847, and the story of the Donner Party spread quickly. Newspapers approached the story from every angle, publishing letters and accounts of those trapped in the Sierra and of those who had rescued them. Eventually, the disturbing story reached Springfield, Illinois; Virginia's second letter to her cousin Mary appeared in the *Sangamon Journal* and was published in other newspapers before the year was out. In 1848, emigration declined considerably.

But the following year, gold was discovered at Sutter's Mill in the Sierra Nevada foothills. More than 100,000 emigrants from all over the world rushed to California over the next two years. In 1850, California entered the union as the thirty-first state.

Those who survived the Donner Party crossing contributed to California's growth. Among them:

Virginia Reed, to her father's dismay, kept her vow and became a Catholic shortly after arriving in San Jose. Two years later she eloped with a much older Catholic man, John Murphy, of whom her father disapproved. Despite her marriage, Virginia remained close to both parents the rest of their lives. She and her husband had nine children. Later in life, Virginia's narrative of her passage to California was published in a popular western magazine. She lived to age eighty-seven.

James Reed recovered his wealth within a few years through various ventures, including gold mining and real estate development. He built a new home and named several surrounding streets after members of his family, including present-day Reed Street, Margaret Street, Virginia Street, and Keyes Street. An enthusiastic supporter of his new state, Reed spent a small fortune lobbying for San Jose to become California's capitol.

Margaret Reed, whom Virginia later described as "the bravest of the brave," gave birth to a son ten months after she and James were reunited, and another son two years after that. She and James took in two of the youngest Donner girls and raised them as their own. The Mason medal she kept for her husband when he was banished from the Donner Party is on display at Sutter's Fort in Sacramento.

Patty Reed married at eighteen and had eight children. When her husband died, she supported her family by keeping a boardinghouse in Capitola. In her later years, Patty gave interviews on her experiences with the Donner Party, and even visited the campsite at Truckee Lake, now Donner Lake, with other survivors. The wooden doll she wouldn't give up is now on display at Sutter's Fort. Patty, who came so close to death in the Sierra Nevada, outlived all her siblings. She died in her Santa Cruz home at age ninety-three.

Tommy Reed grew up and joined his father in his many business ventures. He never married. He stayed close to Patty throughout his life and lived with her in Santa Cruz when he retired. Tommy died in 1915, the last surviving male of the Donner Party.

Leanna Donner lost both parents in the Sierra Nevada, but all her siblings survived. Within a few months of arriving in California, she married another pioneer from Illinois. He built her a home in Jamestown, where she lived to age ninety-six. She and her husband had three children.

Patrick and Peggy Breen settled in San Juan Batista. Patrick Breen became a prominent farmer and community leader. His sons, including **Ed Breen**, made a fortune in the California Gold Rush.

Lewis Keseberg and his wife stayed in Sacramento and had eight more children. Keseberg was the last survivor to be brought down from the Sierra Nevada and one of the few to admit to cannibalism. As a result, he was the party member most haunted by his ordeal. His life was one of lawsuits and failed businesses. He lived to age eighty-one.

Big Bill McCutchen and his wife, whose baby died in the Sierra Nevada, moved to San Jose, where Bill was elected sheriff. Eventually they made their home in Gilroy, where they had four more children.

Mary Graves, John Snyder's sweetheart and one of the few surviving members of the Forlorn Hope, lost both parents in the Sierra Nevada. However, most of Mary's many siblings survived. She became a schoolteacher, married twice, and had seven children.

The ruby pin and other items belonging to Donner Party hero **Charles Stanton** were recovered at Sutter's Fort and returned to his brother and sister-in-law in New York.

Virginia Reed's letter (edited for length) to her cousin Mary Keyes, upon arriving in California:

Napa Vallie
California
May 16th 1847

My Dear Cousan

I take this oppertunity to write to you to let you now that we are all Well at presant and hope this letter may find you all well to My dear Cousan I am a going to Write to you about our trubels geting to Callifornia; We had good luck til we come to ... Brigers ... they pursuaded us to take Hastings cut of over the salt plain thay said it saved 3 Hondred miles, we went that road & we had to go through a long drive of 40 miles With out water or grass Hastings said it was 40 but i think it was 80 miles We traveld a day and night & a nother day and at noon pa went on to see if he coud find Water, he had not bin gone long till some of the oxen give out .... pa got to us about noon the man that was with us took the horse and went on to water We wated thare thought Thay would come we wated till night and ... we took what little water we had and some bread and ... pa went on to the water to see why thay did not bring the cattel when he got thare thare was but one ox and cow thare none of the rest had got to water ... and all of us in we staid thare a week and Hunted for our cattel and could not find them so some of the companie took thare oxons and went out and brout in one wagon and cashed the other tow and a grate manie things all but what we could put in one Wagon we had to divied our propessions out to them to get them to carie them We got three yoak with our oxe & cow so we [went] on that way a while and we got out of provisions and pa had to go on to callifornia for provisions we could not get along that way, in 2 or 3 days after pa left we had to cash our wagon and ... we had to cash all our close except a change or 2 and put them in Mr Brins Wagon and ... we went on that way a Whild and we come to a nother long drive of 40 miles and then we went with Mr Donner We had to Walk all the time we was a travling up the truckee river we met that man and 2 Indians that we had sent out for propessions to Suter Fort thay had met pa, not fur from Suters Fort ... we cashed some more of our things all but what we could pack on one mule and we started (Patty) and James road behind the two Indians it was a raing then in the Vallies and snowing on the montains so we went on that way 3 or 4 days tell we come to the big mountain or the Callifornia Mountain the snow then was about 3 feet deep thare ... well we thought we would try it so we started and thav started again with thare wagons the snow was then way to the muels side the farther we went up the deeper the snow got so the wagons could not go so thay packed thare oxons and started with us carring a child a piece and driving the oxons in snow up to thare wast ... so we went on that way 2 miles and the mules kept faling down in the snow head formost and the Indian said he could not find the road we stoped and let the Indian and man go on to hunt the road thay went on and found the road to the top of the mountain ... and said they thought we could git over if it did not snow any more well the Woman were all so tirder caring there Children that thay could not go over that night so we made a fire and got something to eat & ma spred down a bufalorobe & we all laid down on it & spred somthing over us & ma sit up by the fire & it snowed one foot on top of the bed so we got up in the morning & the snow was so deep we could not go over & we had to go back to the cabin & build more cabins & stay thare all Winter without Pa we had not the first thing to eat … we had that man & Indians to feed well thay started over a foot and had to come back so thay made snow shoes and started again …thare was 15 started & thare was 7 got throw 5 Weman & 2 men it come a stormc and thay lost the road & got out of provisions & the ones that got throwe had to eat them that Died not long after thay started … we had nothing to eat but ox hides o Mary I would cry and wish I had what you all wasted … & we staid at Mr Breen thay had meat all the time & we had to kill littel cash the dog & eat him we ate his head and feet & hide & evry thing about him o my Dear Cousin you dont now what trubel is yet a many a time we had on the last thing a cooking and did not now wher the next would come from but there was awl wais some way provided there was 15 in the cabon we was in and half of us had to lay a bed all the time … and after Mr Breen would cook his meat we would take the bones and boil them 3 or 4 days at a time … we had onely a half a hide and we was out on top of the cabin and we seen them a coming

O my Dear Cousin you dont now how glad i was, we run and met them … thay staid thare 3 days to recruet a little so we could go thare was 20 started all of us started and went a piece and Martha and Thomas giv out & so the men had to take them back … and o Mary that was the hades thing yet to come on and leiv them thar did not now but what thay would starve to Death Martha said well ma if you never see me again do the best you can the men said thay could hadly stand it it maid them all cry … when we had traveld 5 days travel we met Pa with 13 men going to the cabins O Mary you do not nou how glad we was to see him we had not seen him for months we thought we woul never see him again ... he said he would see (Patty) and Thomas the next day ... some of the compana was eating from them that Died but Thomas & Martha had not ate any Pa and the men started with 12 people Hiram O Miller Carried Thomas and Pa caried Martha ...

O Mary I have not wrote you half of the truble we have had but I hav Wrote you anuf to let you now that you dont now what-truble is but thank the Good god we have all got throw and the onely family that did not eat human flesh we have left every thing but i dont cair for that we have got through but Dont let this letter dishaten anybody and never take no cuof and hury along as fast as you can.

Virginia E. B. Reed

AUTHOR'S NOTES

*A*ll *We Left Behind: Virginia Reed and the Donner Party* is historical fiction based on known facts of the tragedy, including Virginia's letters and her memoir, *Across the Plains in the Donner Party: A Personal Narrative of the Overland Trip to California 1846-47.* Special edition of *Century Magazine,* 1891. Reprint, Silverthorne, Colorado: Vistabooks, 1995.

Since this is Virginia's story, I chose to highlight, and in some cases combine, the party members I think most influenced her personal journey.

This book contains several excerpts of Virginia's letters, as well as letters written by James Reed, Tamsen Donner, and Charles Stanton. The complete letters can be found in *Overland in 1846: Diaries and Letters of the California-Oregon Trail. Volumes 1 and 2,* edited by Dale Morgan. Lincoln, Nebraska: University of Nebraska Press, 1993.

Excerpts of Lansford Hastings' descriptions of California are from his book, *The Emigrant's Guide to Oregon and California in 1845.* Santa Barbara, California: The Narrative Press, 2001. Facsimile of 1845 edition.

ABOUT THE AUTHOR

Nancy Herman is a third-generation Californian who is fascinated with her state's colorful history, including the westward migration of the 1800s. She grew up in the coastal town of Watsonville and earned a Bachelor of Arts in Journalism from San Jose State University.

After her 25-year career as a Silicon Valley marketing communications professional, Nancy began researching and writing her first historical novel.

"I drew my facts from diaries, letters, and first hand accounts, including Virginia's memoirs," she says. "Research turned out to be one of the most enjoyable and rewarding aspects of writing this book. Another was following the Donner Party's route by automobile from Independence, Missouri to Sutter's Fort in Sacramento, California.

"I'm in awe of the toughness and determination of our California ancestors who crossed two-thousand miles or more by wagon, on horseback, and even by foot to start new lives here."

Nancy lives with her husband Tom in the Sierra foothills, not far from the site of the Donner Party's 1846-1847 winter entrapment.

Visit Nancy Herman online:
www:nancyhermanauthor.com

Made in the USA
San Bernardino, CA
07 August 2015